I0668675

By Dean Murray

Reflections

Broken

Torn

Splintered

Intrusion

Numb

Trapped

Forsaken

Riven

Driven

Lost

Marked

Left

Dark Reflections

Bound

Hunted

Ambushed

Shattered

Burned

The Awakening

Reborn

Immortal

Endless

A Broken World

The Society

The Destroyer

The Warlord

The Founder

The Outsider

The Desolation

Reflections
(Dean Writing as Eldon)

The Greater Darkness

A Darkness Mirrored

The Compelled Chronicles

Stone Heart

The Guadel Chronicles

Frozen Prospects

Thawed Fortunes

I'rone

Brittle Bonds

Shattered Ties

Immortal

Dean Murray

Published by Fir'shan Publishing

ISBN 978-1-9393635-2-7

www.FirshanPublishing.com

First Edition

For Mr. Winston

You never stopped pushing your students to think outside the box. I didn't feel like I ever really got it while I was in your classes, but somewhere alonge the way something clicked, and I suspect you deserve a healthy amount of the credit.

Chapter 1

"My name is Kyle. Once upon a time I was your husband and you're here right now because I've got a proposal for you."

The words hung in the air between us like smoke that refused to dissipate. The idea of having been married to someone I had no recollection of should have been absurd, should have been impossible, but it wasn't.

I already knew that I'd been married to Jace in my last incarnation. Once I'd accepted that, it was only a tiny stretch to believe that there could have been others, other men whom I'd shared my life and body with.

"When?"

"Three hundred years ago. You were mine before you were Jace's."

"What happened to us? Do you remember?"

Kyle's knuckles went white around the hilt of his sword, but that was the only visible indication of the maelstrom of emotion I somehow knew he was feeling. "I don't remember, but I've read about it in my journals."

"Did one of us die? Is that how we ended up apart?"

"No, at least not the way you mean. You and I were two of the best researchers for more than a hundred years. We pioneered everything from more efficient standing wards to time manipulation. Our knowledge made us powerful, but it also made us tempting targets. At one point, the two of us were cut off from our pantheon and I burned through all of my memories in order to get you to safety."

His story reached out and grabbed hold of me in ways I hadn't expected it to. It didn't make any sense for it to affect me so strongly. This was just another story, just another piece of ancient history. It had happened to me, but it hadn't happened to this version of me, to this incarnation. I didn't remember any of it, but that didn't stop tears from racing down my face.

"What happened after that? Were we separated?"

"No. You spent several months helping me put my life back together, and then you informed me that you didn't want to remarry me. You married Jace and never looked back."

"That's a lie!"

The words jumped out of me of their own accord. The anger that had been bubbling in the back of my mind for as long as I could remember exploded out of its cage with a fury that should have terrified me.

Up until that moment, I would have said that nobody was capable of equaling my rage, but Kyle matched it instantly. It shouldn't have been possible to feel another person's emotions, but I felt his anger reaching out to me, tendrils of white-hot fury that wanted nothing more than to ignite everything around us so that he could step back and watch the world burn.

"It's the truth! You married my brother and the two of you and Kat cast me off without a second thought."

"I refuse to believe that. I wouldn't have just turned my back on someone I loved. That isn't me, not in this incarnation, not in any incarnation. You're leaving something out."

I should have been terrified. Kyle must have fought Fenrir to a standstill. He was obviously an Awakened, one who doubtlessly knew dozens of ways of killing me, but my anger didn't leave any room for other emotions. I matched his anger by fanning the flames of my own.

He raised his hand as though planning on hitting me, and instincts that I hadn't even realized I possessed took over. It was easy to find the heartbeat of this place. The only sound was the low hum of the central air system.

I harnessed my anger, made it work for me instead of allowing it to explode into a consuming fire. The time bend happened instantly. My heartbeat shot through the roof at the same time that the sound of the massive fans slowed to a crawl.

I immediately knew that I'd pushed too hard. I wasn't just at double or triple speed, I was at more than six or seven times normal speed. It was too much, I wasn't strong enough to function at such a high multiple, but even as I realized my error, the augmentations to my physical body dropped into place with solid jolts that were imagined more than felt, and I shot away from the bed moving faster than I'd ever moved before in my life.

If I'd been up against someone else maybe I would have chosen to attack rather than run, but Kyle was more experienced than I was, and regardless of whatever else might have happened in the last few hundred years, at one point we'd meant a lot to each other. I ran, digging deep, throwing myself forward against the resistance of the air that suddenly felt thicker than water around me.

The door was still open, which saved me valuable time, but then my heart stuttered as I saw the stairs awaiting me and realized that I was going to have to make a choice between up or down. Fortunately, one of the side effects of bending time was having a lot more time to think.

I slowed down for only a fraction of a second before realizing that all of the signs pointed toward me being underground. The forced air, the lack of windows, it all said the same thing—I was going to have to go up if I wanted to get away. I turned to the left and headed up the stairs, taking them three at a time.

Traveling at this speed was a new experience in more ways than I'd anticipated. I'd expected the air to resist my efforts, but I hadn't realized that I was going to be able to feel the metal stairs flexing and groaning under my weight. Running on a level surface at even just three or four times normal speed required significant amping to the bones and soft tissue; running up stairs was a whole different ball game.

Ascending at a speed of sixty or seventy miles per hour meant that each step hit the metal underneath me with the force of a battering ram. I was worried that the stairs were going to give way beneath me, but I was too terrified to slow down.

I went up three levels in quick succession before I heard the first sign of pursuit. The big question was how far Kyle had chosen to bend time. He'd started out at normal speed, which meant that I had a significant head start. Even if he'd reacted within a second or two of me making a break for it, my greater speed meant that I had somewhere between a ten and twenty-second head start.

As I felt my body start to go into oxygen debt I told myself that it was going to be enough. It should have been enough—against almost anyone else it would have been. Jace and Kat had both been in agreement that most of the other pantheons hadn't pushed time manipulation research as far as we had.

Two—or even three—times speed was nothing. You could even function at that speed for limited periods of time without amping up your body. It wouldn't be pretty and you'd be nursing bruises and stress fractures for weeks afterwards, but it could be done.

Six or seven times normal speed was like trying to function at the top of Mount Everest. I shouldn't even have been able to manage the series of effects that I'd just pulled off. They'd happened without conscious thought on my part, but that didn't mean that I hadn't noticed just how much more complicated they'd been than what Jace and Kat had taught me.

The muscle amp I knew amounted to little more than just making my body burn the sugars in my bloodstream at a faster rate and forcing my nervous system to recruit more muscle fibers with each movement. That was about the extent of my knowledge of anatomy and physiology, but I'd been able to feel other things changing this time.

My connective tissue, the ligaments and tendons that were a vital linkage in getting the force generated by my muscles down to the ground, had just thickened and transformed to something else, something that was capable of laughing off the abuse I was inflicting on my body.

That alone would have blown my mind, but I'd caught glimpses of other changes. My blood was different, able to clear lactic acid much more efficiently and transport several times as much oxygen. My bones had transformed to something that felt like living crystal, and my skin wasn't just thicker and stronger, it was pulling energy from the heat in the air around me.

I hadn't just amped up my body, I'd transformed it into something that never could have evolved on this planet. That kind of knowledge went beyond just the tricks Jace and Kat had taught me up until now, and it was orders of magnitude better than what most other pantheons were capable of.

Only Kyle wasn't just some other random Awakened. He was a researcher and at one point he'd been part of our pantheon.

I'd started up the fourth set of stairs when I heard it. The stairs back outside of the bedroom rang like a gong. I could feel the oxygen debt start to deepen. The air was so thick that it was hard to get it in and out of my lungs. I was gasping, trying to get fresh air down where it had a chance of doing me any good, but for all of its viscosity going down, once it was down there it felt thin and unsatisfying.

I needed to slow down, needed to back off enough for my system to be able to keep up with my oxygen consumption, but I knew I wasn't going to get another chance to escape. I pushed off the stairs even harder and felt the metal start to tear in the split second before my foot left the next step.

I hadn't just hit the limit of my circulatory and respiratory systems, I'd hit the limit of what the stairs were capable of supporting. My mind was screaming that there had to be a way to go faster, but my thoughts were starting to become more lethargic. I wanted nothing so much as to just drop to the ground and throw up—it was all I could do to force myself to keep moving.

The next set of stairs rang like a gong, but this time there was a cracking sound a second later. He was gaining on me. It shouldn't be possible, but I could hear him closing in.

Up ahead I could see an odd glowing curtain of light positioned a few inches ahead of a heavy steel door. I couldn't explain what I was seeing other than as the result of my brain shutting down due to lack of oxygen.

I blinked, but the curtain of light didn't go away. It didn't matter though, the door was my ticket to freedom. I just needed to drag it shut behind me and then use my limited transmuting ability to fuse the steel into one piece. Kyle would have to slow down and break through the door before he'd have any chance of following me.

"Selene, stop! You're about to hit my ward!"

Kyle's voice floated up the stairs, but for all of his undeniable urgency, it still sounded like it was coming to me by way of a miles-long tunnel. My mind stuttered. The last gong had sounded from only a few feet behind me, but that wasn't possible—he couldn't have made up so much ground—the stairs wouldn't have allowed him to go any faster than I had been, not without giving way.

I was less than a foot away from the translucent wall when Kyle grabbed my arm. It was too late. Our momentum would carry me to the door and let me slam it on his arm.

A fraction of a second later his other arm was around my waist and then he was ahead of me, feet travelling up the curved wall like something out of a science-fiction movie. I would have said that it was impossible to stop two people moving at more than fifty miles per hour before we hit the glowing wall I'd been charging towards.

Kyle proved me wrong. He ran up the side of the wall and grunted as he pushed off against it to stop my forward motion. It felt like I'd been hit by a garbage truck. Despite all of the changes to my system, I still felt my flesh bruise and a jolt of agony shot through two of my ribs as they broke.

I had just long enough to see Kyle's shoes come apart and the concrete underneath his feet start to powder, and then my toes grazed against the shimmering field of light in front of the door and I was thrown across the room.

The last thing I remembered thinking before my head hit the wall was that the glowing barrier must not have been a figment of my imagination after all.

Chapter 2

"Are you done running?"

My eyes were blurry, but I didn't need to be able to see to hear the unhappiness in Kyle's voice. Maybe I should have been scared, but the simple fact that I was waking back up told me that he still wanted me alive. It would have been a lot easier to let me die, but instead he'd nearly managed to keep me from hitting his 'wards' at all.

"Will it do me any good to run?"

My eyesight cleared enough for me to make out his face a few inches away from mine. He shook his head. "No. You don't have the knowhow or power to break out of here. Wards that strong cost at least a full decade's worth of memories to break through."

I wiggled my toes to make sure that the impact hadn't paralyzed me, and then sat up with a grimace. I was still alive, but just about every piece of my body hurt.

"I *am* seventeen. If I wanted to break through your precious wards I have enough juice to do it."

"No. You couldn't. It would take more than a decade of *Awakened* memories. Right now all you've got is a decade and a half of weak human memories. Even assuming you knew how to bring down a set of wards, you could throw everything you had at them and leave yourself as blank as the day you were born without bringing them down."

He was wrong. I couldn't explain why, but I was different than all of the rest of my kind. Somehow when I'd been Awakened *all* of my memories had taken on the vibrancy and hard edges that were part of being an Awakened—even the memories from before I'd manifested my power.

I was twice as powerful as he had any right to expect. I was still ridiculously outclassed, but at least I had that working in my favor.

I looked back up to find Kyle watching me with a suspicious look. "I don't know what you're planning, but it won't work. Even if you somehow manage to bring down the ward you can see, there are several more wards that you'd have to destroy before you'd be able to escape."

"I'm not planning anything."

That earned me a smirk. "I may not remember our time together, Selene, but I wrote down your tells just in case we crossed paths again. You're planning something—you can't help it, it's in your nature."

"I don't know what you're talking about."

"Did Jace already tell you about wards? That's surprising given just how little time the two of you have had together, but I guess it's not out of the question. If you're thinking that killing me will bring the wards down, you should know that these wards don't work like any other wards you've learned about. If I die they still won't come down. They'll stay up forever."

That made something inside me bristle. "Nothing is forever, Kyle. If you die the wards will come down. They are strong, so it may take a while, but they'll start fading as soon as you're not around to serve as an anchor."

To say I was shocked didn't even begin to do what I was feeling justice. I had no idea where those words had come from, no explanation for what I'd just said. I looked at Kyle, half expecting to see him overcome by anger again, but he was smiling.

"That's very good. I have to admit to being impressed. Everyone else believes that the location serves as an anchor, that all the wards need from us once they are established is a kind of low-level power feed that is the next best thing to undetectable. I wasn't aware that Jace was a good enough researcher to have figured that out."

I almost told him that Jace hadn't, but at the last second I realized that I needed to play my cards close to my chest. I'd been giving too much away for free.

"So why don't you tell me why it is that your wards are so much different than everyone else's."

"They are different because I'm the only one—other than Jace apparently—who's experimented with them during the last few hundred years."

"And you discovered…"

"I discovered that over time the wards naturally take a shape that is perfectly stable, a shape that doesn't need outside power to maintain it, a perfect matrix that actually draws energy from the air around us."

"How come nobody else was able to figure that out before now?"

"Because the shape is too complex for inferior minds to grasp, too complicated for what most pantheons consider researchers to understand."

"Wow, you don't have a pride issue—not at all."

Kyle smiled again, but this time it didn't make it to his eyes. "I don't believe in sins, but even if I did, pride wouldn't make it on my list. Most of the ills of the world can be directly traced back to people's refusal to admit that all men are not created equal. Some men—and women—have ability, but most don't. Some individuals are capable of great things, but most will spend their entire lives trying to justify their existence, trying—and failing—to create value in excess of their consumption."

I half expected Kyle to break out into maniacal laughter, but he met my gaze with eyes that seemed as sane as any I'd ever seen.

"So what, the rest of us are just insects that should serve as your slaves?"

"No, you—and apparently my brother—are more than that. You're capable of true greatness, capable of seeing beyond the falsehood of human philosophy. You may not see it yet, but eventually you will. People talk about equality, but the truth is that as long as individuals are different with regards to their capabilities, the only way to create equality of outcome is for the gifted to serve as the slaves to the drones."

Chills ran down the outside of my spine. There was something familiar about Kyle's arguments, something seductive.

"You would reverse the slavery, put the weak and simple under the lash and destroy human choice."

My words came out lacking the condemnation I felt like they should have carried, but I wasn't sure whether that was because I hadn't had a chance to think about them, or if it was because I didn't actually believe what I was saying.

"Exactly. It's always going to be a matter of slavery, Selene. Us or them, there isn't any middle ground. Someone has to serve and someone has to rule. It only makes sense for the most gifted to be in the driver's seat."

"I don't believe it has to be that way."

That earned me another frown. "I should have known better than to expect real discussion out of you. Once upon a time we were able to have real conversations about this topic, but you no longer have the framework for real thought."

"Tell me then. Why does one group have to be in charge? Why can't everyone just do their own thing?"

"Because nobody is willing to let the law of consequences naturally play out. As long as we're not willing to let people starve to death there are only two possible outcomes. Either you make them slaves and force them to earn the bread they need to survive, using them as dumb animals guided by your intellect, or you make yourself a slave and bind yourself to feeding those too stupid or lazy to sustain themselves."

I wasn't sure that I even understood what Kyle was saying. I'd never had a philosophy class, never thought about anything more complicated than how I was going to make it to college, but what I did understand of his arguments was disturbingly close to what I saw going on in the world around me.

Slavery had been outlawed for ages and yet my dad spent nearly every waking hour working in the Conners' tile factory, making huge profits for Sandra's dad. In a lot of ways my dad would have been better off as a slave. The way things were going right now he was probably only a few years away from a heart attack. If Mr. Conner had owned my dad he probably would have made sure that my dad was taken care of. A slave couldn't work after they were dead, and they weren't free to replace. If an employee died, all you had to do was send a card to their family and hire a replacement.

I didn't want to believe that the world was as terrible as Kyle had made it out to be, that things were as black and white as he was saying, but no matter how hard I tried I couldn't come up with a reason he was wrong.

I looked away—unable to argue, but unwilling to agree—and felt him lean forward to press his advantage home.

Before he could say anything, alarms started ringing all over the room.

Chapter 3

The alarms nearly made me jump out of my skin. I opened my mouth to scream for Kyle to turn them off, but he already had his phone out and a couple of taps shut the alarms down.

"What was that?"

"It was my intruder alert system."

"Wait, you mean some poor idiot is trying to walk off with your silverware?"

"Hardly. No common thief would get far enough to trigger my alarm. Whoever set my sensors off has already made it through a ward that is strong enough to knock a normal person unconscious."

"So it's an Awakened then?"

I tried to keep the hope out of my voice, but I wasn't very successful. Kyle looked up from his phone and shook his head at me. "It isn't Jace and Kat, if that's what you're hoping for, but yes, it's either an Awakened or one of the fae."

"How do you know it isn't Jace? I can probably convince him not to hurt you if you let me go now..."

Kyle waved away my implied threat without even a hint of concern. "I'll never understand what it is that my brother does to engender such blind confidence in his capabilities. Didn't it even briefly occur to you that Mephistoles might have killed Jace?"

"Wait. Is Jace okay? Did Kat and Ari survive?"

It actually *hadn't* crossed my mind, but the panic I felt at the idea was almost uncontrollable. I started to pull myself to my feet. It was silly, I wasn't going to be any more capable of getting past Kyle's ward now than I'd been the last time, but I was desperate to do *something*.

"Yes, as much as I'd like to say otherwise, all three of them survived. Kat was badly injured in the fight with Fenrir, but she had enough emotional juice left to get your sister to a cave and heal herself before losing consciousness for several hours while she regenerated most of her abilities. Jace had several close calls, but he was ultimately able to disengage from his fight with Mephistoles. The last time I checked he was tracking Kat and Ari down."

"So it could be the two of them here to rescue me!"

"Your knight in shining armor isn't on his way, Selene. Even assuming that the two of them had any idea where to find my home, it wouldn't matter. They aren't strong enough to get past my wards, not in anything remotely approaching a reasonable period of time."

Kyle tapped on the screen of his smartphone and then held it up. "Just in case you need some additional proof, here's the video feed."

The footage was the same grainy black-and-white video surveillance I'd seen in spy movies, so it took me several seconds before I could decipher what I was seeing. The person walking along at the front of the group could have been anyone, but there wasn't any mistaking the massive, four-legged form following along behind him.

"That's Fenrir. Only he's smaller than when I fought him."

"Yeah, killing one of the fae is a lot harder than killing one of us. I cut his head off, but that just meant that he disappeared and reappeared a little while later. I cost him some of his power and size, but he's still incredibly dangerous."

"So what, he can't be killed?"

Kyle grabbed my shoulders before I could take a second step towards the door and the ward that had thrown me across the room.

"I said he can be killed. It's just complicated. Taking down a fae requires killing them multiple times until they become weak enough that they can't continue to hold their shape. It doesn't happen often, but it does happen."

If I'd been with Jace I probably would have already been crying on his shoulder, but Jace wouldn't have manhandled me like that. Kyle's hands on my shoulder just made me angry.

"Then why the hell didn't you finish the job back in the mountains? What kind of idiot leaves something like Fenrir alive to come looking for payback?"

"The kind of idiot who knows he can't go head to head with Mephistoles."

"What are you talking about? Jace stood up to Mephistoles. The two of you could have easily put Mephistoles down and then made sure that Fenrir was gone for good."

The glare I got from Kyle should have started me on fire. "Jace didn't stand up to Mephistoles, he distracted him for a few minutes while the rest of you ran. No one person stands up to Mephistoles."

"Fine, but it wouldn't have been just you, it would have been you *and* Jace."

"You're in over your head, so I'm going to make a few things clear. First, I don't help Jace, and I especially don't help Jace take down someone who's been a thorn in his side for the better part of a hundred years.

"Second, I'm not normally on the opposite team from Fenrir. Trying to take him all the way down wasn't anything remotely approaching a sure thing, and if I'd tried and failed then all I would have done is guarantee that he'd have it out for me. This way there was at least a chance that he'd be willing to let it go in return for some kind of moderate reparations."

"You're scared of him…"

"Of course I'm scared of him. There's a reason why Fenrir was the Big Bad in Norse mythology. He's so old that nobody has any idea who created him, and he's one of the top two or three most powerful members of the Unseelie Court. Nobody tangles with Fenrir if they can avoid it, not even the Lady of the Lake."

"Well, it looks like your plan failed."

Kyle pulled me around by my arm and all but dragged me over to the shimmering veil of his ward. "Maybe, maybe not. Come on, it's time to go see what they're planning on doing."

The closer we got to Kyle's ward, the more my anger turned to fear. I tried to pull away, but he was either a lot stronger than he looked or he was still at least partially amped up.

"Stop writhing around or you're going to end up bumping into the energy field again, and this time I won't bother putting you back together again—assuming there is anything left of you after hitting the wall while completely unamped."

That made me stop, but it didn't do anything about my racing heart or the way that my legs had started shaking. Kyle reached forward and sank his hand into his ward. He wasn't the kind of person to make mistakes, but that didn't stop a tiny voice in the back of my mind from screaming that he was about to be shot across the room.

For several seconds, nothing happened, and then a slight ripple shot out from the point where Kyle was touching the ward.

"Okay, I've rekeyed it so that you can come and go through this one. Don't get any ideas about running though, there are more wards between here and the surface, and even if you get past all of the rest of the wards you'll still have Fenrir and Mephistoles waiting for you on the other side of the last ward."

Kyle didn't seem like the kind to lie about something like this—if he'd wanted me dead he could have achieved his purpose simply by not healing me after the last time I'd encountered his ward. Everything that had happened so far pointed towards him wanting me alive—right now at least—but I still moved hesitantly.

I brought my left hand up and touched the ward with the tip of one finger. It wasn't until my finger pierced the plane of the ward that I realized I'd been holding my breath.

Kyle sighed impatiently and then pulled me through the ward. "Come on, it's not a short trip."

Once we left the bunker, our surroundings took my breath away. The tunnel waiting for us immediately after the heavy metal door, quickly gave way to something I could only describe as an underground city. That wasn't the right word for what I was seeing, but it was the best I could come up with. There were large, open spaces that were much larger than anything I would have expected to see underground.

The ground under our feet was an oddly uniform textured rock—as though someone had decided that normal stone was too slick for their purposes and proceeded to remedy the issue. I caught only glimpses, stumbling in the darkness until Kyle stopped and conjured a fist-sized ball of white light above our heads.

I got the impression that he'd somehow bottled up a chunk of air and then put the molecules in a state of extreme excitement, but knowing what he'd done didn't mean I could replicate it.

"What is this place?"

"It's the world's greatest cemetery."

That forced a shiver through me. "What do you mean?"

Kyle looked frustrated, but rather than just pulling me along like I'd expected him to, he stopped and ran his hand through his wavy, dark hair in a gesture that was disturbingly like something Jace would have done.

"The truth is I'm not sure—all I have is theories. I found it a hundred years ago by following Native American legends of a people who had withdrawn from the rest of the world, a people with great power and knowledge…"

"They were Awakened."

He nodded. "Yes. It actually explains quite a bit. I've always been intrigued by the fact that the mythology in North America is so monotheistic. The people who lived here believed in spiritual totems like the bear or the eagle, but they never set those totems above the great creating spirit that they believed ruled everything.

"South America was a different matter entirely. Down there all of the records point towards a number of different pantheons, but it's as though for thousands of years there were no Awakened anywhere on the top half of this continent."

I cleared my throat. "You said that you had theories…"

"Yes. I think that the Awakened on North America chose to withdraw down here. Maybe they were pursuing some kind of higher state of existence, maybe they just wanted to hide their existence and powers as much as possible from the humans around them. All I can tell you is that they locked themselves away down here and then at some point all died."

My shivers were back. "You weren't kidding when you said it was a giant graveyard. What on earth would make you want to build your home down here?"

"Knowledge. Knowledge is the one thing that drives someone like you or me, Selene. Before they died, this group—this pantheon—made some very interesting advances. This place is a goldmine. The prototypes they created are still far short of what I someday hope to manage, but they got me started down paths I otherwise might not have ever discovered."

"Prototypes of what?"

For a second I almost thought that Kyle was going to respond, but then he looked around and shook his head. "Not here. I'll tell you more when we're safely back inside my bunker."

"Why not just tell me now? It's not like there's anyone around to overhear—this place is nothing more than a giant ghost town—"

Kyle grabbed my arm and whipped me around. "You shut your mouth. If I tell you we aren't going to talk about it, then you'll listen or I'll leave you here by yourself to stumble around in the darkness until you either starve to death or run into Fenrir and Mephistoles."

His voice came out as little more than a hiss. It didn't make sense—very little that had happened since Jace and Kat had arrived in my life made sense—but I could tell that I'd pushed him too far this time.

"You won't do that. You need me."

"Need is a relative term. I saved you from Fenrir and brought you here because I think you could be useful to me, but I'm not going to let you ruin everything by bringing the Unseelie and Seelie courts both down on my head."

His grip tightened to the point where he drew a gasp out of me. He was hurting me now, and there was something in his eyes that didn't look entirely sane.

"I'm sorry, I won't say anything else."

"That's right. You can speak when spoken to, but otherwise keep your mouth shut. Bringing you here has already cost me more than I expected it to. Don't make me second-guess the decision or I might just give you to Fenrir in the hopes that will be enough to get him off my back."

I nodded as silent tears trickled out of the corners of my eyes. Kyle released me and stalked off, leaving me to choose between following or staying in the darkness by myself. As much as I wanted to stay where I was, or even better to attempt to retrace my steps and seal the door to his bunker behind me, I knew it would take only seconds for me to become completely disoriented. My best bet was to follow him. He was right about one thing.

Knowledge was what I needed if I was going to get out. For now at least, knowledge was the thing that was going to drive me.

Chapter 4

We walked for more than fifteen minutes and passed through a number of additional wards before finally coming to the outskirts of the city. At each ward we went through the same routine. Kyle grabbed me by the arm as he reached for the ward and then once he'd rekeyed the field, I passed through unharmed.

The final ward was different. I could see the lights that Mephistoles had brought from more than a hundred yards away. The presence of someone who wanted me dead was a momentary distraction, but even that couldn't tear my attention away from something else that I'd noticed as we'd gotten further and further away from Kyle's bunker.

There was an odd shimmer to the air that I couldn't explain. It was moving, so it couldn't be a ward, but I had no idea what else it could be. It was like there was this shimmery, floating gauze that kept pace with us in fits and starts. One moment it would be scant inches in front of Kyle, and then a split second later it would jump forward so that it had encapsulated a section of ground twenty feet ahead of us.

The way it was moving was odd enough, but even more unusual was the way that it seemed to make everything on our side of the moving line more vibrant while washing out the colors of everything on the other side.

As we finally arrived at the last ward I couldn't keep my question inside for any longer. "What..."

I stopped after just one word because Kyle had already turned around with a glare that told me there would be consequences if I didn't keep my mouth closed.

The indistinct figures on the other side of the ward finally approached close enough that I was able to make out the dark sheen of Fenrir's coat and the unsettling gray eyes of his Awakened companion.

"To what do I owe the pleasure of this visit?"

Kyle's voice was dead in a way I'd never heard out of anyone before. We all knew that Mephistoles and Fenrir had come to extract their pound of flesh, but Kyle might have been discussing the weather in some remote location he never expected to visit.

Mephistoles turned out to be a tall, skinny man who looked like he was at least seventy. He moved more easily than I would have expected out of someone of his apparent age, but seeing him still made me glad that I was one of those people who awakened at a younger age.

Mephistoles looked at Kyle with bitter gray eyes. "You interfered with our attempt at capturing those journals—don't tell us that you didn't. That's obviously her standing at your side."

"I deny nothing, Mephistoles. Our arrangement came to an end almost two decades ago. I stayed out of things while your pantheon killed Selene's last incarnation. There was nothing in there about me standing to one side while you attempted to kill her again."

The fear that had been foremost in my emotions was suddenly buried under a tidal wave of anger. Whatever crimes I might have committed against Kyle surely couldn't have merited him agreeing to stand to one side while Mephistoles hunted Jace, Kat and me.

More than anything else, I wanted to shove Kyle through the ward, to push him out to where Mephistoles and Fenrir could take him down. I didn't move though. The situation was too complex. Killing Kyle was the kind of thing that couldn't be undone and I knew it would be better to wait until I knew more about what was going on.

"And me, darkling? What is your rationale for striking me down?"

Fenrir's voice was deeper than I'd expected it to be. He pressed right up to the edge of the ward as though emphasizing that he wasn't scared of it, wasn't scared of us.

"My apologies, great one. If there had been another way I would have taken it, but—at least for now—Selene is under my protection. You'll notice I didn't use any more force than absolutely necessary to accomplish my ends. You and I both know that you could have been robbed of much more power than you were if I really wanted to ruin things between us."

Mephistoles laughed, a harsh, grating sound. "You have an awfully high opinion of yourself, whelp."

"No more so than is merited by my actual capabilities."

As Kyle spoke he turned to one side, finally making the sword at his side visible. Mephistoles went white as soon as he saw the weapon. "Why didn't you tell me he had that?"

Fenrir apparently took exception to his erstwhile ally's tone. He didn't turn completely away from us, but he growled at Mephistoles and fixed the old man with a threatening glare.

"Don't question me. I had no way of knowing that Kyle had the sword. He struck me down too quickly for me to register anything. I wouldn't have even known it was him if not for the fact that I recognized his scent when I rematerialized."

Mephistoles grabbed hold of a heavy necklace of silver links that had been concealed beneath his robes. "Don't threaten me. He may have the sword, but I'm not without advantages of my own. You don't want to sour this relationship, not now that you know what you're up against."

Now Kyle did smile. "That's the thing about advantages, my friends. Not all advantages are created equal. This particular advantage is at its finest when dealing with a longer term. Just how long do you think it will take you to break down this ward? Two days? Three?"

Mephistoles' smile didn't make it to his eyes. "I can handle anything you want to throw in my direction for three days. Besides, it might take Fenrir working by himself three days to kick the doors to your little castle down, but if I help out it will go much quicker than that."

"Indeed, but then what will you do about the wards that are waiting behind this one?"

Fenrir growled. "You're bluffing. If you had other wards we would have been able to feel them."

"Ah, but that's the thing about wards. They get used so rarely that nobody has done any research into them for hundreds of years. These wards aren't what you're used to. Think about it. Normally you would have been able to sense this ward even before you crashed through my first line of defense."

I could see the realization dawning behind Mephistoles' eyes.

"You figured out a way to use a weaker ward to mask the presence of a stronger ward behind it."

"Indeed I did."

Mephistoles took a step forward and raised his hand, resting it just fractions of an inch away from Kyle's ward. "Then you're a bigger fool even than I realized. Now that I know that's a possibility it's just a matter of time before I figure out how to replicate what you've done. I'll be untouchable."

"I think you overestimate your intellect, old man. You've always been at your best when scavenging through someone else's trash. This particular trick is going to take decades to unlock."

"Time is the one thing I have plenty of."

"Not if I kill you first."

Even as the words left Kyle's mouth he shot forward, moving so quickly that he disappeared. It was like he flickered out of existence and then reappeared standing in front of Mephistoles. Kyle reached forward, obviously intending on pulling Mephistoles into the ward, but the older man was already moving backwards.

Kyle's hand snapped shut on empty space and a split second later a blast of lightning tore through the air. Everything was happening so quickly that for a second I wasn't sure who had attacked whom.

It wasn't until the lightning discharged its fury against the ward that I realized Kyle had defended himself simply by stepping back behind his defenses. I was still trying to adjust to the sudden outburst of violence when Fenrir threw himself into the ward as though trying to get through so that he could tear my throat out.

Fortunately the ward was strong enough to repel the attack and it threw him back into the wall with enough force to shake the floor.

Despite all of the shocks to my system, my anger hadn't gone anywhere. I reached out to the heartbeat of my surroundings, keyed in on the crackle as the ward continued to discharge the energy it had just absorbed, and slowed the crackle down to a hum. Kyle was still moving several times as fast as I was, but now I could at least follow the fight.

As I began amping myself up, Kyle stepped back through his ward and cut loose with a bar of white-hot golden light. I'd expected him to attack Fenrir while the gigantic wolf was still reeling from its encounter with the wards, but instead Kyle targeted Mephistoles.

It was the same attack that I'd seen Kat use to destroy trees like they were nothing more than twigs, but Kyle's beam of light was an order of magnitude more powerful. It should have vaporized Mephistoles and gone on to bore through the rock wall behind him, but instead it simply stopped, disappearing inches before it struck his body.

Kyle stepped back through the ward a split second before Fenrir threw himself at the ward again. This time I was amped up enough that I was able to see the ward deform. Fenrir's jaws closed only inches away from Kyle's head before the wolf was once again thrown clear of the cerulean field.

"You failed, Kyle. You can't fight both of us, not forever. Eventually you'll be half a step too slow and one of us will manage to cut you down."

"I don't fail. I accomplished exactly what I intended to accomplish, old man. Your ability to negate my sun lance is impressive, but we both know doing so isn't cheap. You just burned a peak memory. I can't imagine that you have too many of those."

"Now you're the one who's underestimating me. My...advantages are such that stopping something like that requires nothing more than base memories. I do hope you didn't waste one of your peak memories, infant."

Kyle's smile got even bigger. "All the better. How much did you lose just now? A month, two months? You just finished torching the mountainside in a failed attempt to kill my do-gooder brother. How much did that cost you? A year? Two?"

"I've got enough reserves to squash you like a bug."

Kyle shrugged. "Maybe, maybe not, but the real question is if I'm the one you should be worrying about. Jace and Kat have to be smarting from the beat down you just administered to them. If I were you, I'd be a lot more worried about what they're going to be doing back at your place while you're stuck here for the better part of a month trying to kick my doors down."

"The two of them don't have a chance in hell of breaking my wards."

"Maybe, but who's to say that it will be just the two of them? The location of your lair is hardly a secret. Everyone knows where it is, they just know that it would take more than a day or two to breach your wards, and they don't want to tangle with you."

"I need the girl."

"That's uncommonly dense, even for you. You don't want the girl, you want her research journals. Those are with Jace and Kat, not with us."

Mephistoles paused as though thinking about what Kyle had just said, and Kyle used that fraction of a second to attack. He darted through the wards again, sidestepped Fenrir's lunge, leaped over a blast of fire that left his clothes smoking, and stabbed Mephistoles through the shoulder with the sword that had spent the entire fight up until now sheathed at Kyle's waist.

The scream that tore free of Mephistoles' throat raised the hair on the back of my neck, but his obvious pain didn't slow him down much. A sword that looked like it was crafted out of strands of black light materialized in Mephistoles' hand and he made a savage cut at Kyle's neck that should have taken off his head.

Mephistoles was obviously amped up to at least four or five times normal speed—he was fast enough that I wouldn't have been able to evade his attack, but Kyle was faster than me. I expected him to block the black sword with his silver one, but instead he sprinted towards the closest wall and ran up it, throwing himself backwards in a flat trajectory that took him over Mephistoles' sword.

Fenrir was moving much slower than I remembered from my fight with him, but even so he'd had enough time to spin around and charge back towards the other two combatants. I stepped towards the fight, desperate to do something to help, but the ward still hadn't gone anywhere.

I was forced to watch as Kyle spread his arms in opposite directions and sent another beam of golden light at Mephistoles while slashing Fenrir across the face with a strike so fast that his sword was nothing more than a blur even to me.

Mephistoles once again dispelled Kyle's attack, but this time the force of the beam sent him staggering back several steps. More astonishing though was the black blood flowing across Fenrir's muzzle. The cut wasn't enough to stop Fenrir, not when he was out for blood. The dark wolf didn't even slow, but it was in that precise instant that Kyle's genius was fully revealed.

Fenrir's teeth once again snapped shut on empty air and then he clipped Kyle with his shoulder, sending him careening through the ward and across the stone floor. I feared for a second that Kyle had cut himself on his own sword, but a couple of seconds later he pulled himself back to his feet and saluted both of his opponents.

"Thanks for the warmup. I promise I'll be back whenever you least expect it to continue what we just started."

Kyle shuddered slightly and then slowed down until he was moving with nearly the same languid torpor as the other two. I was still amped up, and for the briefest of moments I was tempted to charge him. I didn't know the first thing about combat, but as Kyle had just demonstrated with Fenrir, if you were moving at seven or eight times the speed of your enemy you had an advantage that was hard to overcome.

I had a good chance of coming out on top. Kyle was already breathing hard from his exchange with Mephistoles and Fenrir. I wasn't stupid enough to think that he'd exhausted his emotional reserves or his memories either one. But he was too close to me to amp himself back up before I could land my first blow.

I could feel the decision balance on the edge of a knife and then I took a deep breath and released all of my effects. I had no delusions regarding my ability to take on both Fenrir and Mephistoles. It was still possible that killing Kyle wouldn't result in his wards fading away, but even if he'd been lying that didn't change the fact that Fenrir and Mephistoles would be waiting for me once the ward came down.

I was wasting memories and emotional strength that I might need later on.

"Come on, Selene. It's time to go back and fix ourselves something to eat."

Chapter 5

The walk back to Kyle's bunker was a quiet affair. We crossed back through the eerie halls and spaces without incident, and then Kyle led me down the stairs until we arrived at a level even further down than his bedroom.

Saying I was shocked at what I saw next would have been an understatement. Rather than the dark, damp dungeon that I'd half expected him to throw me in, I was instead gifted with a vista that was nothing but bright light, greenery and dark, rich soil.

"A garden?"

"Yes, a garden. I was serious when I said that we would be coming back to get something to eat. Here that means more than just sticking something in the microwave—that means picking the food and washing it before sitting down to prepare it."

He looked at me and cocked his head to one side. "You seem surprised."

"I guess I am. I never would have guessed that this is what I would find down here."

Kyle shrugged. "It was the only logical thing. When I found this place I knew that I needed to keep a low profile. I worked with some of the best architects money could buy for nearly six years to design somewhere I could disappear, a sanctuary where nobody could ever find me. Power, water, food, it all had to be addressed before we moved the first shovelful of dirt. My electricity comes from a pair of heat-driven turbines that tap into a hot spot in the earth's crust thousands of feet further down."

I took another step into the massive, circular space and gloried in the feel of the lights on my skin. It wasn't sunlight, not quite, but it was close—close enough to chase away the chill that had been a part of me ever since I'd opened my eyes in Kyle's bed.

Kyle let me twirl with my eyes closed for several seconds before continuing. "The level above this one is full of waste treatment equipment, there are two separate wells that draw clean water up to the bunker and every single mechanical component has redundant backups in place that should be sufficient to last at least another forty years."

I stopped spinning and opened my eyes. "But why? What purpose does all of this serve?"

"It let me keep the city above us a secret and it made it so that I could research in peace. It gave me a chance—at least temporarily—to bow out of the unending fight that is part and parcel of life up there."

"Wow, I wouldn't have thought you were the type. This seems a little—well, I guess…back to nature for someone so determined to enslave everyone in the world. I would have thought that it would eat at you to have to spend hours every day maintaining equipment and growing your own food. You seem more like the type to have a huge staff taking care of every possible extraneous bit of your life so that you can concentrate on your research…"

Kyle reached over and took a heavy black bag off of a shelf near the door. "You're missing the point. It's not about turning people into slaves, it's about establishing a new order. It's about ending the pointless wars between the pantheons. It's about making society truly fair for the first time ever."

"Oh, that makes all the difference. I can totally see how I misjudged you now. You're totally the kind to spend half your day growing organic food and the other half writing your manifesto."

"Sarcasm doesn't become you, Selene. You're better than that."

"Really? I'm having a hard time believing that. I kind of like sarcasm, but if I'm really 'better than that' then you'd be answering my questions rather than just filling me with more of your political BS."

"You didn't ask a question. You made an observation."

I shot him a dirty look and just waited. For a minute I thought I wasn't going to get an answer. He walked over to a patch of dark soil and began digging into it with his hands. After just a few seconds of effort he came up with several large potatoes.

"Researching doesn't work like that. Sitting in front of my chalkboards for hours doesn't necessarily translate to advances. Real creation almost always happens while the inventor is doing something else. My brother worships something that men have defined as being bigger than the whole world but yet still small enough to fit in your heart, but the truth is that the subconscious is the true creator. All I can do is provide it with as many truths—as many of the pieces—as possible, remove any unnecessary distractions, and then it's up to my subconscious to come up with the solutions I need."

"This is just about cutting yourself off? It's all just so that you don't have any distractions?"

"No. Safety is a prime consideration, as is maintaining the secrecy of the prototypes I found in the city up above. There are many things that played into my decision to come down here. I'm not the first though. It's happened dozens of times over the thousands of years of our existence.

"At some point the true men and women of the mind retreat away from everything else. They withdraw, just like the Awakened on this continent did, in an effort to push forward the frontiers of knowledge. Humans can get away with a lesser degree of separation, but that's never the case for us. If we stay where others of our kind can get to us, we eventually end up pulled back into the conflict."

"So what happened to the ones before you? If that's the solution to all of the problems in the world how come everything that needs to be known hasn't been discovered a thousand times over?"

"They failed. Secrecy is never enough. Eventually someone always stumbles upon their retreats and they never even see the attack coming. Sometimes they opt for wards, but without my most recent round of discoveries there isn't a way to create a ward that is both strong enough to serve as a significant deterrent and weak enough not to serve as a gigantic signal fire to everyone within a few hundred miles that there is something valuable there."

"That's it? You figured out everything?"

"Yeah, basically. At least it was working up until recently."

Kyle walked over to a tomato plant and sighed as he picked three large specimens off of the vines. "I'm so close. I thought I was close even before I came here, but the pantheon that lived in the city above us knew things. They were close to inventing actual artifacts, so incredibly close. I just need a few more years and I'll be able to change everything."

"What's an artifact?"

He didn't look up from his bag. I waited, but he simply moved on to a plot of onions.

"Kyle, what's an artifact?"

"I guess your education is less complete than I was expecting it to be. Come on. Everything else I need is already upstairs in the refrigerator. Let's go eat."

Chapter 6

Dinner was surprisingly good considering that Kyle made everything from scratch from what he was able to grow downstairs in his garden. If the food exceeded my expectations, the conversation was even sparser than I'd expected it to be.

We'd finished eating and I'd cleaned up before Kyle finally spoke to me again.

"I take it that you've decided against killing me?"

"What makes you so sure?"

His smile this time had an element of exhaustion to it that I hadn't been expecting. "I saw you thinking about it next to the last ward before you finally let your time manipulation drop."

"I guess not. It's tempting, but I'm not sure I'd get away with it. Besides, even if I did kill you, I'd still have to worry about Mephistoles and Fenrir."

"Maybe, but maybe not for much longer."

"What do you mean? Do you have a plan that would let you kill both of them?"

"Now you're giving me too much credit. I'm not capable of taking both of them on."

I fought back a yawn. It didn't make sense. I'd just spent who knew how many hours unconscious—there was absolutely no reason for me to already be tired. I was only supposed to need a few hours of sleep per night.

"So what did you mean then?"

"I mean with any luck we won't be dealing with both of them for very much longer." Kyle walked over and took me by the arm, pulling me to my feet, but this time the motion was almost gentle. "Come on. You're exhausted."

"I don't understand why."

"You just burned several days' worth of memories at the very least. Actually, it's even more likely that you burned a couple of peak memories to make it happen. Sustaining that level of time bend isn't the kind of thing you should be doing lightly. It will be less of an issue as you get more experience and are able to isolate the drain so it's just taking memories rather than tapping into the rest of your system as well, but for now that kind of expenditure will leave you exhausted."

I was so tired that I let Kyle lead me downstairs to his bed without complaining. I was already in bed and only a couple of breaths away from unconsciousness before I realized that it should have creeped me out to be sleeping in the bed of someone I didn't trust.

I woke up an indeterminate amount of time later feeling much better. I used the gigantic white marble bathroom and then slowly made my way to the stairs. I already knew what was in the bottom two levels, but I didn't know what was directly below the bedroom.

I debated calling out for Kyle. This was a shockingly huge installation to find underground, but there was a decent chance that he'd be able to hear me if I stood in the stairwell and yelled. In the end, my curiosity won out.

Despite all of his threats and rough treatment, some crazy part of me wanted to trust Kyle. It made absolutely no sense, which meant that it was probably some kind of leftover feeling from one or more of my past incarnations.

Based on everything I'd been told so far, that shouldn't have happened. Jace and Kat had been in perfect agreement that it wasn't possible for an Awakened to bring knowledge from a past life forward to another incarnation. I didn't doubt that they'd been telling me the truth as far as they knew it, but I was becoming more and more sure that there was something else going on, something that they didn't have any experience with.

I'd been learning things much too quickly, but that was nothing compared to having amped my system in ways that nobody had ever taught me. I didn't know how, but somehow I'd carried something across the barrier of death. That had to be the reason I was so inclined to trust Kyle, but it didn't mean it was a good idea to act on the inclination.

I walked down to the level just above the waste reclamation equipment, and carefully pulled open the heavy door. The room behind the door was full of equipment, fertilizer, seeds and everything else required to keep the bunker in working order. I took a quick loop around the level in case Kyle had secreted something important down there with all of the spares, but the truth was that I didn't even know what I was looking for.

I was more than a little disheartened as I pulled the door closed behind me and started up to the next level. I started to open the door— pushing it forward—and then at the last second I recognized the characteristic shimmer of a live ward.

I pulled my hands away from the door like I'd been scalded, relieved that I'd managed to avoid crossing the plane of Kyle's defenses. Interesting. I'd been surprised that Kyle had taken me down to his bedroom and left me unattended not just once, but twice. I'd been wondering if that was some kind of sign of trust, but apparently he didn't trust me any more than I trusted him. He just knew that everything he valued was safely secured behind a ward that I didn't have the ability to bring down.

I looked at the door for several seconds before gingerly reaching up and spinning the big wheel that locked it closed.

There was a secret here. More than likely it had to do with Kyle's research, now I just needed to decide whether it was safe to ask him about it. Probably not.

I headed back up the stairs, passing the bedroom level and not stopping to open any of the closed doors until I was nearly up to the top level where the kitchen and living room were located. Surprisingly enough, the door to the second to last level wasn't shut. I was starting to realize just how badly my little snooping expedition downstairs could have gone, but I couldn't help myself. I took a deep breath and then stepped across the threshold.

I felt a flicker of surprise as I took in the comfortable space arrayed in front of me. If the top level was the formal receiving area—not that Kyle actually entertained—then this was the family room.

One entire side of the room was taken up with a massive exercise area, everything from free weights to stationary bikes and wrestling mats. Another quarter of the space was dedicated to a large metal desk, an array of computer equipment, and several floor-to-ceiling book-cases.

The last quarter of the circular space included a small kitchenette, a couch, and a television that had some kind of gaming system hooked up to it. The most surprising thing of all was the fact that Kyle was sprawled out on the couch, asleep.

I walked over, taking care to avoid making noise, and reached down to cover Kyle with the blanket half-draped over him. A second later I found myself on the floor with Kyle kneeling on my chest, his hand around my throat.

"What were you doing?"

He relaxed his grip around my neck just enough to permit speech. I was shaking, but I managed to get an explanation out.

"You were cold—I was going to move your blanket so that you weren't so uncovered."

"Are you sure you didn't decide this was your chance to end me?"

"No, I decided against killing you—remember?"

Kyle's eyes were deep pools and I was drowning in them. It was different than how I felt when I looked into Jace's eyes, but it was just as strong. Whatever I'd felt for Kyle back in the day must have been incredibly intense.

"Did you?"

"Yeah. I did."

It wasn't like I could have said otherwise—not when he was half a heartbeat away from crushing my throat—but as the words tumbled out I realized they were true. I couldn't have said exactly why I'd decided against killing him, but I had.

Kyle looked into my eyes as though trying to weigh the truth of what I'd just said. I wondered if he had amped up his powers of observation, if he was paying attention to slight changes in my respiration and pulse. It was possible, but I hadn't caught any trace of an effect. He seemed to be gauging my sincerity the old-fashioned way.

It didn't make sense. Jace had said that any given Awakened was doing well if they managed to hold onto a hundred and fifty years' worth of memories.

Kyle had spent the last several decades locked away inside his bunker. It was possible that his isolation had allowed him to burn fewer memories than our contemporaries, but I'd gotten the feeling that Jace and I had been together for something like two hundred years.

Maybe I was off on the timeline, maybe Kyle did somehow remember our time together. It was unlikely, but there certainly seemed to be something behind his eyes, something that said he knew me better than I knew myself.

"I almost believe you, Selene."

"Well, I'm sorry that you're one of those people who have a hard time accepting the truth."

My response was more sarcastic than I should have risked, but I couldn't seem to help myself. Amazingly, he smiled rather than getting angry.

"Maybe I was wrong about you. The sarcasm fits you better than I'd realized."

He let go of my throat and shifted so he wasn't on my chest anymore. I slowly sat up, never taking my eyes off of him. It was like being caged with a wild animal. There was no telling what he was going to do from one moment to the next.

"Great, so now that you're starting to believe me when I say that I'm not going to kill you, can we start talking about you letting me go?"

"My letting you go wouldn't make any difference, Selene. As long as Fenrir and Mephistoles are out there, I'm just as much a prisoner here as you are."

"For some reason I'm having a hard time buying that. The only way that would be true is if you are willing to let me leave once it's safe for me to do so. Otherwise I'm a different kind of prisoner than you are."

He hadn't blinked while I was talking. Normal people blink. It should have been creepy that he wasn't, but it somehow didn't bother me. Instead I got the feeling that he was forcing himself not to blink because he didn't want to miss out on anything I was saying. It was like catching every change in my expression was a survival-level need. Like it was as important to him as breathing.

I swallowed and told myself that I was misreading the signs. It was all too ludicrous to believe.

"I've learned that it's foolish to rely on the future unfolding a certain way, Selene. This conversation is pointless. We can discuss it again if we manage to take care of our unwelcome visitors."

He stood and offered me his hand. I almost took it. It would have just been one person helping another person to their feet, but it didn't feel like that was all it was. It felt like that would be a betrayal of everything I had with Jace.

I expected Kyle to lash out when I didn't take his hand. His fingers curled into fists as I used the couch to get back to my feet, but he didn't yell. He just turned away from me and walked over to his desk.

"I think you're probably going to want to see this."

"See what?"

He didn't answer. Instead he just sat down at the desk and started clicking away on the mouse. I waited for several seconds hoping that he would thaw and tell me what I was in for, but it was like I'd ceased to exist.

I finally walked over and stood behind his chair so I could watch the monitor. As soon as I was in position behind him, he started the video that he'd queued up while I was walking over.

"What am I looking at?"

"Video feeds. The bottom one is just behind my first ward, the one that keeps everyone from being able to detect the stronger wards behind it."

"The one that they took out on their way in?"

"Yeah. The feed on the top is the second ward, the one where we fought them a little while ago."

"You mean the one where *you* fought them."

Kyle's hand tightened slightly on the mouse, but he just nodded wordlessly. The video was playing by at four times normal speed, but not much seemed to be happening. Several seconds went by before I saw Fenrir wander back into the field of view.

It was hard to say for sure on such a grainy, black and white image, but it looked almost like he'd gotten bigger since we saw him last. Fenrir shook himself as though psyching himself up, and then leaned into the ward. The cameras weren't capable of detecting the ward, but they were able to pick up the discharge of power as the ward tried to throw Fenrir into the rock wall behind him.

"What's going on?"

"He's draining the ward. It's dangerous, even for a fae as powerful as Fenrir, but he already took the measure of my defenses earlier during the fight so he knows it's not powerful enough to destroy him instantly. That means if he's careful he can cause it to discharge power without triggering it fully. It's painful, but each time he presses up against the ward he absorbs part of the energy that is discharged."

"You mean he's using your defenses to get stronger?"

"Yeah. That's the other reason why turtling up hasn't ever worked for very long. Erecting wards is a good deterrent for other Awakened and for weaker fae, but they're like a nine-course meal for the more powerful fae."

Kyle had slowed down the footage as Fenrir touched the ward, so I was able to count the seconds until the massive wolf stumbled away from the wards and collapsed against the far wall. A moment later, a shadow detached itself from the wall. Mephistoles stepped forward and shot a bolt of light at the ward that caused the feed to stutter. By the looks of things, he'd very nearly burned the camera out.

"They're working together to try to bring down the ward?"

Kyle nodded as the image from the camera started to coalesce back into something other than white snow.

"More than that, it looks like they managed to take it down."

He brought up two more feeds with a couple of clicks as I realized that I couldn't see any sign of Mephistoles and Fenrir at the second ward.

"I thought you said it would take them two or three days to bring it down."

"Yeah, I did say that. It appears that I underestimated just how desperate my taunts would make Mephistoles to get back to his lair."

"So what, we've got three days now before they'll have taken all of the remaining wards down and then we're screwed?"

"Just watch."

Kyle sped the feed back up to the point where it only took a few seconds for the two intruders to make it onto the third feed. At that point he slowed it down slightly, but the two of them still moved with a speed that would have been comical if not for the fact that every second that passed brought them that much closer to knocking on our front door.

I watched Mephistoles gesture repeatedly at the ward before Fenrir finally edged into the ward and then stumbled away with his fur smoking.

"The third ward is more powerful than the other two?"

"Yes. There is only so much you can do to hide the effects of a powerful ward inside of a weaker ward, but distance helps a lot. The first ward was really just designed to mask all of the other wards. The second ward was meant as a deterrent. Only someone who was really determined to get at me would go to the trouble of taking the second ward down, so the third one is as strong as I could make it without having it burn through the masking effect of the first two wards."

I was only listening with half an ear. The rest of my attention was glued to the video feeds, but even so I felt like I must have missed something when I saw Mephistoles turn and walk away.

"Wait, what's going on?"

Kyle didn't answer. Instead he sped the feeds back up for several seconds before slowing them back down to regular speed.

"There, that should do it."

"Do what?"

"Just watch."

Even as the words left his mouth I saw what it was he wanted me to see. Mephistoles appeared on the first feed, the one that watched the location where the first ward had been positioned. He appeared, walked through the tunnel and disappeared.

"Wait, he's gone?"

"Yeah, it sure looks that way. I'll know for sure once I'm on the other side of the third ward and can sense his presence—or lack thereof."

"But why would he do that?"

"Because the stronger Mephistoles gets, the more fearful he becomes."

That one left me scratching my head, but apparently seeing half of our competition leave had Kyle in a good mood.

"Mephistoles is a third-rate researcher. He's smart, but he's missing the spark that would let him really accomplish something. Fortunately—or unfortunately, depending on how you look at it—he's figured out his limitations. He stopped trying to do real research centuries ago. Instead he's become one of the world's foremost thieves of real research. He's long since identified everyone with any real ability and he stalks them. He lives in constant fear of someone else realizing that he's not home and breaking into his lair so that they can steal all of the research journals he's amassed."

"That's why he was after Kat and me eighteen years ago…"

"Yes. It was common knowledge that you and I were the two who pioneered time shifts. You were brilliant and powerful, but you only had Kat and Jace supporting you. The three of you were staying mobile, but even so you were at the top of a very short list of targets. If you'd been younger and less powerful he might have tried to capture you, but you weren't. He wanted your journals, but you were too careful for him to steal them while you were still alive."

"So he killed me."

"Yes. To be honest I was surprised that you didn't manage to at least take him with you."

"That's why you agreed not to interfere. You thought he and I would kill each other off and that would leave you perfectly positioned to take over everything."

There was something in Kyle's eyes that I couldn't read. In someone else I would have said it was regret, but there was no trace of anything like that in his voice.

"Yes. That was my plan exactly. I figured that once you and he were both dead I could swoop in and take your journals and with a little bit of luck get my hands on the knowledge he's spent the last few centuries looting. Then I could disappear down here in my refuge for however long it took for me to solve the problem I've been working on."

"Do you expect me to be okay with that, Kyle?"

He shrugged—which just made me angrier.

"I'm dead because of you."

"Except you aren't dead. You're standing here next to me."

I wanted to hit him.

"*I'm* standing here, but I'm not the same person. The other version of me is gone—because you killed her."

"I didn't kill her."

"You're arguing semantics. If you hadn't given Mephistoles your blessing he wouldn't have come after me."

Kyle turned his chair so he was facing me and leaned back so he could look me in the eyes without bending his neck.

"There isn't any way to know that for sure. My withholding my blessing from Mephistoles might have made him back off, but it might not have. He might have gone after you anyway—or even worse, he might have come after me."

"And that would have been worse?"

"Yes."

I gave him the kind of sugary sweet, totally insincere look that I'd always hated so much from Sandra. "I rest my case. You agree that you dying is a bad thing—you can't be mad about me being bent out of shape when it was *me* who ended up dying."

"You're missing the point, Selene. What does it matter if one of us dies? You, me, Jace, Kat, the end result is the same. We come back. We don't stay dead, we don't remember the pain."

"That's the point! Dying deprived me of memories, memories I no doubt valued."

"Did it? Those memories would have just been fodder for some fight."

I opened my mouth to tell him he was wrong, but there was something in his eyes that stopped me. This wasn't just an argument to him, this was his religion. A religion of facts and logic, but a religion nonetheless. I wasn't equipped to fight this fight. Not anymore.

"I don't know why you're wrong, but you're wrong."

"Am I? I ask it sincerely. I've looked at that problem again and again. What are we but a collection of memories? Memories that we routinely sacrifice for terribly small ends. If we aren't snuffed out at the time of death, what have we really lost—what thing of substance have we been deprived of?"

"You're skating on very thin ice, Kyle."

He gave me a sad smile. "That's what you said to me when you abandoned me and threw yourself into Jace's arms. At one point those words would have ignited a terrible rage in me, but the memory of that time is long gone now. All I have left of it now is journal entries."

I wasn't sure if I wanted to slap him or hug him. He looked like a lost little child, but he also looked like an arrogant demigod who was far too powerful and callous to be allowed to meddle in people's lives.

In the end I chose neither course because I realized he'd given me the answer I needed to refute his argument.

"It was wrong because you deprived me of all the things I could have accomplished during the last eighteen years. You talk of nothing but your precious research, but what about my research? Who knows what I could have accomplished?"

"That's just it, Selene. All of the signs indicated that you lost the gift after you left me. You dumbed yourself down to Jace's level so that he wouldn't feel threatened by you and you've spent every year since then doing nothing more than refining the research that you and I had already pioneered together.

"I had to balance your limited, shrinking contributions to the world against what I could potentially accomplish over the next several decades. I had to weigh the loss of your memories against the knowledge I was uncovering in the city above us. I had no choice but to choose the way I did."

"You had no right."

"I not only had the right, I had the obligation."

I slapped him and then I turned and walked out of the room.

Chapter 7

I couldn't have said what instinct caused me to go up rather than down when I hit the stairs, but a few minutes later I found myself in the kitchen, where I cried for nearly an hour.

More than anything I just wanted to be back home with the people who I knew loved me. My dad, Ari, Kat…Jace. I had only Kyle's word that they were all okay, and that was scant comfort given that he was cold-blooded enough to let Mephistoles kill me in return for a few more decades of undisturbed work.

As much as I worried about what was going to happen to me, I was even more worried about my friends and family. It had been long enough now that my dad knew I'd disappeared. I was sure he was freaking out with worry.

The best possible situation was that Jace and Kat had told him what was going on and that I'd been abducted while fighting a figure from

Norse mythology, but even that wasn't a very good outcome. Poor Jace. He and my dad would both be blaming themselves for what had happened to me, and while they were both powerless to find me right now, I suspected that was going to be a hard thing for Jace to acknowledge. Jace was used to being in control of his surroundings—sitting around, passively waiting for some kind of ransom note wasn't going to sit well with him.

Every single person I loved was worried about me, and my only solace had been the fact that at least Mephistoles and Fenrir had both been focused on Kyle and me. If Mephistoles had really left, then my family—new and old—was in danger again.

I heard Kyle start up the stairs about the time I finally cried myself out. By that point I had nearly pulled myself back together, but even if I hadn't, I would have forced myself to put on a convincing show. I wasn't going to let Kyle know how much he was getting to me.

I'd spent the last few days worrying about the fact that Jace and Kat were convinced that I was their golden ticket to safety. I hadn't felt anything like the smart, tenacious woman they'd described, but they'd nearly convinced me despite all of my doubts. Having Kyle tell me that I'd been nothing more than a flashy façade wasn't exactly going to help me sleep at night. It was like he'd picked out my single biggest vulnerability and jammed a knife into me.

"What do you want?"

"Come on. It's time."

"Time for what?"

Kyle didn't look back. I watched him disappear past the ward without any kind of response. It was the ultimate game of chicken and I blinked first.

"I'll stay here—I really will!"

"Fine, but just so you know, the computers are all locked down—you can't use them to get hold of anyone."

I realized I was gritting my teeth, but I forced myself to my feet and hurried after Kyle. The last thing I wanted to do was lose him and end up lost out in the abandoned graveyard he was so excited about.

"You're really not going to tell me what's going on?"

"Nope, it's best if you're surprised."

"Best for who?"

"Best for me, obviously."

Kyle didn't seem at all worried about being overheard this time around—apparently his earlier concerns had just revolved around the subject matter. That little tidbit of information probably would have been a lot more helpful if not for the fact that I still didn't understand what it was we'd been talking about on the way out the last time we'd left his bunker.

Fenrir was waiting for us as we walked around a corner and stepped into another large open space.

"Back so soon? You must be nervous at just how quickly we were able to breach your first two wards."

"Not at all. I came back to see if you've come to your senses yet."

Fenrir's voice had been a menacing rumble, but it was nothing compared to his growl. "The last petty god who insulted me lost much more than just his hand. You're treading on dangerous ground. I was already planning on killing you, but if you push me too far the death you'll receive will be much more painful than it needs to be."

Kyle's smile didn't reach his eyes. "No offense was intended. I was merely trying to point out that you're by yourself now. You've crashed through my first two wards, but they were never meant to stand up to someone like you. This ward, however, is an altogether different proposition, as I'm sure you've realized."

Fenrir growled again, and this time it felt like the stone underneath our feet was shaking. Kyle just smiled again.

"Obviously it's not strong enough to keep you out forever—I'm not sure that anything other than Camelot is—but up until now I've been very careful not to make this personal. In the last fight I didn't even mark you except for that one time at the end. Do you really want me to come at you with everything I have?"

"I'm singularly unafraid of you, Kyle. You would have to get lucky again and again to permanently kill me, while all I have to do is have one good day to get you out of my hair for the better part of two decades."

"You're sure, Fenrir? You've absorbed a fair amount of power from the two wards you've already taken down. I'm willing to let bygones be bygones. You can walk away now and not have lost much of anything in the grand scheme of things. I won't make the offer again."

"You're wasting your breath. Go back to your hole and get the rest you're going to need in order to come out and challenge me again. We both know that you're still too exhausted to face me right now. I warn you though that by the time you get back you'll be up against more than just me again."

"Oh? Is Mephistoles coming back?"

"No, that useless bag of bones won't be back until he smells blood in the water and figures he has a chance of swooping in and taking the pretty bauble hanging from your hip, but he promised to send some of my brethren to help me."

"And you believe him?"

"Of course. If he doesn't come through then I'll be camping in front of his door rather than yours."

All of the back and forth between the two of them was dizzying. Even so, it wasn't in my nature to just sit passively back. I opened my mouth to interject something sarcastic, but before I could get the words out Fenrir hit me with the last thing I'd been expecting.

"Oh, by the way, he wanted me to make sure that the two of you knew that he and his most recent skirt got hold of your girlfriend's father. Even if you have some kind of bolt-hole it's not going to do the two of you any good. Mephistoles is going to eventually get her old journals—that or he'll kill all of the humans that she's become attached to over the last couple of decades."

I felt like I'd been punched in the stomach. I was having a hard time breathing, and the world had gone all blurry around the edges. That didn't stop me from taking a step forward though. It was stupid, there wasn't anything I could have possibly done against Fenrir with my bare hands but the rational, thinking part of me wasn't in charge right then.

The tide of anger that broke over me stole away my reason, which was exactly what Fenrir had been hoping for. I was only inches away from the edge of the ward when I felt a surge of power. A split second later something shoved me hard enough to knock me to the ground.

Kyle had used the distraction I'd provided to bend time and amp his systems up to full combat readiness. He pushed me back away from the ward and then charged through with the point of his sword leading the way.

It was like watching a fight in choppy stop-motion animation. Kyle was so fast that I caught only flickers of motion when he moved. Fenrir was completely outclassed in the speed department, but it was almost like he could sense what Kyle was going to do before he did it.

Kyle would streak in and slash at Fenrir and then he'd dart away, often only centimeters ahead of Fenrir's massive, rending teeth. Within a couple of seconds Fenrir was bleeding from no less than six different wounds. None of them were life-threatening, but they were all significant.

I finally came back to myself enough to bend time to the point where I could keep up with the fight, but I didn't try to stand, didn't try to go help. It was obvious that Fenrir's description of the situation was more on point than I'd realized.

It was almost possible to convince myself that Kyle was just toying with Fenrir. Nearly every time he charged in he scored some kind of strike on Fenrir. It was tempting to think that a heartbeat's extra effort could have turned any of the attacks into something fatal, but I could see the expression of concentration on Kyle's face.

He was...scared wasn't the right word. He was conscious of the fact that he had much more to lose than Fenrir. All it would take was one mistake for him to put himself in Fenrir's power.

The difference in their speed meant that he could continue to have his way with the massive beast as long as he did everything perfectly, but one trip, one hesitation, one overreach would be all that it would take to flip the tables around.

It was the kind of high-stakes gambling that made the games they played in Vegas look like child's play, and it absolutely took my breath away. Kyle was nothing less than amazing, and for the first time I realized something that Jace and the others had been trying to tell me.

Speed was an incredible advantage, but speed could only buy you so much. Past a certain point all it did was give you more time to think about what came next. Kyle had amped his body up to a superhuman point, but even his new strength and durability had limits. He was moving at a speed that made even simple air resistance feel like a thousand pounds of force pushing against his every motion.

It was like a lethal game of chess. Both of them knew the other's capabilities well. Fenrir knew that he could withstand a tremendous amount of damage, and he knew that Kyle was limited not just by his strength, but also by the traction of the rock under their feet. Kyle had put on a new set of shoes sometime since my aborted escape attempt, but these new shoes were already showing the strain of trying to keep up with forces that no shoe designer could have anticipated.

On the other hand, Fenrir's paws seemed to individually have less grip than Kyle's shoes, but Fenrir had four points of contact to Kyle's two. That meant that Fenrir was capable of abrupt, violent changes in direction that Kyle couldn't match—at least not in the long term.

Both combatants moved with a complicated grace that I was starting to realize was more about positioning their bodies and weapons in such a way as to limit their opponent's options while simultaneously giving themselves as many routes forward as possible.

Kyle drifted slightly closer to the back wall than normal, and Fenrir suddenly surged forward, using his vast bulk in an attempt to force Kyle back into a corner where he'd be at the wolf's mercy. I felt my breath catch. I was sure that the fight was over, but Kyle's expression never even flickered.

I heard a dull ripping sound as one of Kyle's shoes gave way beneath the titanic force he subjected it to, but it had lasted just long enough. Kyle spun out of the way of Fenrir's lunge and sank his sword into the beast's side.

I expected the blow to drop Fenrir in his tracks, but instead he threw himself to the side, trying to crush Kyle against the wall. Kyle dropped to his knees, one hand still on the hilt of his sword, and Fenrir's bulk sailed over his head.

The collision when Fenrir hit the stone wall was breathtaking. I was so distracted by all of the dust falling down from the roof of the cave, and the high-pitched yelp as Kyle's sword was driven in even deeper, that for a second I didn't register the snap that indicated Kyle hadn't managed to get away completely unscathed. As Fenrir bounced away from the unyielding stone, Kyle reached up with his left hand and pulled his sword free.

Fenrir spun around, snapping at Kyle, but the big wolf had ended up too far into the corner where the two walls met and that slowed him down just enough that Kyle was able to stagger through the ward to safety.

Fenrir's roar was so powerful that I thought for a moment that he'd deafened me. The dark wolf threw himself at the wards with such force that this time he was launched across the cavern, hitting the stone wall with a sickening crunch.

I thought for a second that Kyle would charge back out and finish Fenrir off once and for all, but when I looked over at him I realized that his right arm was broken in at least two places. He was doing his best to look unaffected by what had just happened, but his skin was paler than normal.

Fenrir levered himself back to his feet and his eyes were bright yellow pools of hate. "How are you doing that? None of your kind should have those kinds of emotional reserves. Mephistoles, yes, but that's entirely due to the bauble around his neck. You should have run out of steam only seconds into that fight!"

"And yet I didn't. Instead I came very close to destroying your form again. I failed, but in this instance, even failure is a kind of success. With more of your kind on their way you can't afford to just let the damage I did heal normally. You'll trade some of your strength to speed your natural healing. I suspect that I just undid most of the gains you made by dropping my first two wards. Imagine what I'll do over the next couple of weeks."

"It's impossible!"

"Apparently it's not."

Chapter 8

Kyle didn't sag until we were well out of sight of Fenrir. Even then he would have still kept walking under his own power if not for the fact that I took his undamaged arm and looped it over my shoulders. I wasn't sure that I was doing any good, but I couldn't just watch him suffer and not help.

I got a reserved, but appreciative smile from Kyle in return for my efforts, but he didn't say anything until we were back to his bunker and I'd pushed the heavy metal door closed.

"You do realize that there isn't anything keeping you here, don't you? I rekeyed all of the wards but the second one to allow you through them. Now that the second ward is down you could make a run for it if you wanted to."

"I...well, I guess I hadn't thought about that."

Kyle shrugged with just his left shoulder. "If you try to make a run for it Fenrir will still chase you, but if you'd amped up your speed and stamina and then waited until he and I were in the middle of our fight you would have had a pretty good head start."

I considered what he was saying for several seconds before shaking my head. "No, it's a nice thought, but I don't know how to get out of here. Even if I made it past both you and Fenrir I'd still just be lost inside this creepy abandoned city."

"There's a notepad downstairs on my desk. Go grab it and I'll draw you a map. If you head back out now there is a chance that Fenrir will still be injured. That should buy you an extra mile or two before he catches up with you. There's a highway off to the east. With a bit of luck you should be able to flag down a car and hitch a ride. Once you're in a vehicle he won't be able to keep up for long."

I wanted to take Kyle up on his offer, wanted to go get the paper he would need to draw me a map, but I kept coming up with other problems. I didn't know how to create light, which meant I'd be running in the dark. I didn't know what the temperature outside was like—for all I knew we were in the middle of Alaska and I'd freeze into a solid block of ice before I made it to the highway.

"No."

"Fair enough. You'll be better off waiting until I tangle with him again before making a break for it. There's a chance that his friends will have arrived by then, but if they haven't then you'll be almost guaranteed to make it. I suggest shooting for a time bend that is about four times normal speed. It won't buy you as much of a lead, but I think you'll be able to sustain that all the way to the road."

"I'm not going."

I wasn't sure what I was expecting. Surprise maybe? Whatever it was I was hoping for I didn't get it. He just cocked his head to one side.

"You're not?"

"No."

Kyle gritted his teeth while he shifted his broken arm closer to his stomach. "Do I get to know why?"

"Shouldn't we do something about your arm?"

"There's a splint in the cabinet over there. It's not as good as the stuff a couple of levels down, but it will do the job for now."

"For now? Can't you just heal it? I saw Jace heal something when we were back at the lake…"

"Yes, my brother has always been very good at healing effects. Unfortunately, taking care of light burns is not nearly as complicated as fixing broken bones. Normally I can still manage it, but after that last fight I'm too emotionally depleted to manage anything of the sort. I'll set the bones, splint them, and then take enough pain medication to put me under for three or four hours.

"That should be long enough to regenerate some of my emotional vibrancy, but not so long that my body's natural healing process will have had much of a chance to kick in. It's an unfortunate injury in many respects. I'd hoped to get at least one more fight in with Fenrir before his friends arrived. Things will be much more difficult once I'm outnumbered again."

"How are you doing this?"

Kyle had been looking at the cabinet where he'd indicated the first-aid supplies were located, but now he looked back at me. As astonishing as it was that he was continuing to function despite the pain he was in, it was even more incredible how little his face gave away. I had absolutely zero idea what he was thinking other than that he wanted that splint.

"Doing what?"

"Working so many powerful effects so closely together. I know basically nothing about your world—our world—but Fenrir is right. Nobody should be able to do what you just did."

"Are you asking me, or are you telling me?"

"Telling?"

Kyle took a deep breath. "I'm not entirely opposed to explaining, you'll need to answer my earlier question. Why are you choosing to stay here rather than trying to run away again?"

My first instinct was to just shrug and try to deflect his question again, but I knew that wasn't going to work. Kyle wasn't going to tell me what I wanted to know unless I gave him a real answer.

I was trapped by my own hunger for information. I suspected that this was the way that Kyle was most comfortable functioning. Nothing for nothing, valuable information in return for valuable information.

"Fine. I'm staying here because it feels like the right thing to do. I hadn't really thought it through enough to put names to everything until you forced me to, but if I run then the best-case scenario is that I end up back home with Jace, Kat and my sister."

"That sounds like a good thing..."

Kyle's response made me roll my eyes at him. "Yeah, except for the fact that Mephistoles will still have my dad. I don't know anything about where my dad is being held. Maybe Jace and Kat could get him out, but if I go back home it won't be the three of us against Mephistoles, it will be the three of us against Mephistoles *and* Fenrir. I already know that's a fight we can't win."

"So you're staying with me out of pure self-interest."

"Yeah. I guess. I mean you could argue that I'm doing it because it's what's best for my friends and family, but yeah, in the end I'm staying here because it has the best chance of getting me what I want. Does that mean you're not going to tell me?"

"Quite the contrary. An arrangement where both parties are getting equal value out of it is the safest kind of relationship. Get me the splint and I'll answer at least some of your questions."

A few minutes later I had the splint wrapped around his arm and had braced myself with his right hand in both of mine and my feet against his armpit.

"Okay, go ahead and pull on my arm until it straightens out and the bones are realigned."

"Should I amp up my strength?"

"Not unless it becomes unavoidable. There isn't any point in risking additional damage to the limb."

I nodded and then started pulling. Kyle didn't have the same kind of bulky muscles that made Jace so mouth-wateringly yummy, but he was surprisingly strong. I was pulling with everything I had but I still hadn't felt the bones slide into place.

"How good is your fine control when it comes to amping, Selene?"

"Um, good?"

"That's not exactly reassuring…"

"I've been working effects for something like two days. I barely know which way is up at this point."

Kyle broke out into a cold sweat from the pain, but he managed to bite back the scream that I knew had to be trying to force its way out of him.

"Fine. At this point you're able to recognize wards. Have you noticed the ward-like field that follows us around when we get out to the outermost wards?"

"What? What does this have to do with anything?"

"You asked for me to explain some of the discrepancies that you've noticed so far. Do you want to hear the answer, or not?"

"Really? Now?"

"I'm too strong for you to set the bone. I'm trying to distract myself so that you have a fighting chance."

I felt like he was saying I was just another weak little girl. I wanted to argue with him, but I was pulling with everything I had and so far I hadn't managed to make any headway.

"Fine. Distract yourself. I've seen the field you're talking about. It's like everything on our side is super vibrant, and everything on the other side is washed out and dreary."

"That's it. It moves in fits and starts."

"Yeah, I've seen it."

"That is something that nobody else has ever managed. I've created a field inside of which time moves at double speed."

He said it with such obvious pride that for a second I thought he was pulling my leg. "You just finished telling me downstairs that you and I pioneered the first time bend something like two or three hundred years ago..."

That earned me a dirty look. "It's not even remotely the same thing. The time bend that you and I researched doesn't do anything to the actual flow of time. All it does is change our perception of time."

"No way. That can't be right. If that was the case I wouldn't get out of breath so quickly."

"Fine, if you want to be technical about it the underlying effect also serves to soup up our muscles slightly, but all of the modifications are purely internal."

I tried to finish straightening my legs, but he was still resisting me too much. There was a little more give to his arm now, but it still wasn't the same thing.

"Okay, I see what you're saying. So how is your latest mumbo jumbo different than that?"

"Surely even in your current state you're intelligent enough—"

I relaxed my body slightly and then jerked on his arm like I was trying to rip it out of its socket. I caught him completely by surprise and his bones slid into place with a disgusting, grinding click.

Kyle had gone white and his smile was shaky, but he managed to reach over with his left hand and pull on the straps that tightened the splint down to the point where it had a chance of keeping the bones in place.

"I should have known that you were dissembling."

"Yeah, that's me. Masterful dissembler girl. So you've found a way to speed up the actual flow of time, so as far as Fenrir and the rest of the world are concerned we are recovering our emotional reserves twice as fast as we should be."

"Yes, exactly—that's not all though. We're also accruing baseline memories at a much faster rate than our contemporaries."

"That's brilliant. Why didn't I think of that? Even with the old-style time bend that would be a great way to make sure that I got more memories faster than everyone else."

Kyle finished tightening down the splint and then shook his head. "No, it would never work. Creating a time-amping effect burns memories too fast. You would always come out behind where you'd be if you just allowed everything to happen at its normal speed. Time amping is only effective if you've got a specific time-bounded objective that you're trying to accomplish."

Something about what he'd just said didn't ring true to me. I tried to think back to my early experiences bending time. Measuring time when you were functioning at two or three times normal speed was kind of a subjective thing, but I'd been sure that I'd come out slightly ahead as far as the time experienced versus the memories consumed.

I thought about challenging him over it, but then I remembered that I was apparently experiencing memory loss in a different fashion

IMMORTAL

than most of our kind did. It was possible that Kyle was wrong, but nobody had ever been able to measure the memories involved with enough accuracy to arrive at any kind of definitive conclusion. Given that, it was a lot safer to avoid the confrontational route.

I forced myself to smile. "Nice, you've renamed the old stuff time amping and the new effect time bending?"

"Yes. The most difficult part of everything is dealing with problems created when you have one contiguous block of material which is aging at different rates. That's why the field moves around in such an erratic manner. It's compensating by only moving along existing faults where the temporal differences won't create problems."

"You make it sound like it's self-aware."

"I guess you're right. I'd never thought about it in quite that fashion." Kyle looked away from me for several seconds and then sighed. "As much as I would like to continue this conversation, it would probably be best if I took that pain medication and got some sleep. Functioning at twice the normal speed has huge benefits for us, but we're going to need to push ourselves or we aren't going to have any chance of beating Fenrir."

Kyle rolled back up to his feet and then walked over to the kitchen. Ten minutes later he was passed out on the couch.

I hadn't bothered to get up off of the floor. I just sat there and watched him for another twenty minutes. I wasn't sure exactly what was going on, but I was positive that I'd just been lied to.

Chapter 9

Once I finally got to my feet I wasn't sure what to do with myself. Kyle was asleep, so in theory I had the run of the entire bunker—other than the section that was sealed off with wards—but that didn't amount to much.

I didn't particularly feel like heading downstairs to his bedroom. I'd be able to read his journals if I went down there, but I just couldn't bring myself to invade his privacy like that. Kyle had kidnapped me, but he'd also saved my life, Kat's life, and Ari's life before he'd brought me here.

Kyle was no saint, but if he was to be believed, at one point we'd loved each other desperately. Apparently I didn't want to risk burning bridges—even when I didn't remember creating the bridge in the first place.

That left the garden—which was a bad idea given that I was more likely to pull up the vegetables by accident than I was to pull up weeds—one of the storage areas, or the office and workout area downstairs. Actually I probably could have stayed up on the first level—a heavy metal rock concert probably wouldn't have pulled Kyle out of his drugged slumber—but I wanted to put some distance between us.

Poking into all of the boxes and spare equipment felt particularly pointless, so I ended up down in what I was starting to think of as Kyle's office. It wasn't any less impressive the second time around. The exercise equipment was dated and the furniture looked like it had seen some heavy use, but all of the electronics were much too new to fit together with the timeline Kyle had originally tried to paint.

He hadn't been locked away down here for the last thirty or forty years—he'd been out shopping as recently as the last year or two. I wasn't sure what to make of that. Was that an outright lie or was it just a detail that he'd failed to include?

I wandered over to the computer and confirmed that it was locked with some kind of password. Someone with more experience and knowledge probably could have figured out a way around Kyle's cyber-security, but I didn't even know where to start.

From there I headed to the mats and ended up stretching for an hour or so. It wasn't the kind of thing that I normally did, but my body had been through a lot over the last little while.

Kyle had apparently healed most of the worst of the damage both from my fight in the mountains with Fenrir and from tangling with Kyle's ward, but the healing effect had still left me feeling tense and stiff.

Once I was done stretching, I headed over to the big bookshelves, but Kyle's taste in books ran mostly to non-fiction. There were a few classic novels, but nothing that really reached out and grabbed me.

I ended up over in front of the DVD collection—which was further proof that Kyle hadn't been locked away like I'd initially thought. The movies weren't all that new. The newest one I could find was about a year old, but the selection was broad enough that I was able to find a romantic comedy that I'd only seen once before.

I was on my third movie when I finally heard movement out on the staircase. A flash of worry shot through me, which in turn just sparked more of the anger that I'd spent so much time lately trying to keep locked down.

I wasn't going to scurry around like a mouse caught in the middle of the floor when the lights came on. If Kyle came in and got pissy about the fact that I'd been down here 'unsupervised' then I was going to give him a piece of my mind.

I heard him pause outside of the door to my level, but I wasn't about to acknowledge his presence, and he didn't venture inside. He continued on downstairs a few seconds later.

Once he was safely out of earshot, there was every reason to relax, but instead I found that I couldn't pay attention to the movie.

Instead of watching the two main characters work through the misunderstanding that had kept them apart for the last half hour, I found myself listening for him, wondering what he was doing.

It didn't make any sense. I'd spent nearly my whole life steering clear of guys. I'd never understood why other girls my age had spent so much time obsessing over one guy or another, but now I was doing it. First with Jace, and then with Kyle.

The two situations were different—obviously. I was in love with Jace. Whatever was going on with Kyle wasn't love. Maybe it was some kind of Stockholm syndrome thing. He had the power of life and death over me, so it was only to be expected that I would be hyper-aware of him, of what he seemed to be thinking or feeling, but that didn't mean that I had to like it.

Honestly, I would have traded away a lot in order to have a bit more of my normal detachment right then. At this rate I was going to have ulcers in just a few days.

I sat there with the movie playing, the volume down so low that I should have just muted it, and listened to the silence from the stairwell, the silence that told me Kyle wasn't nearby. Several minutes later I heard him come back by my level, this time heading up. Unlike the time before, he didn't slow outside the door to the office level. He went straight up to the top level, and then pulled the door shut behind him with a clang.

It took another half hour for the movie to wrap up. I kept thinking that I was going to get up and put another one in, but I didn't. I couldn't seem to find the energy—instead I just sat there and watched the title screen loop endlessly through the cutesy little animation that had gotten old by the second time around.

An hour after I heard Kyle head up to the top level, he finally came back down the stairs. I grabbed the remote and started the movie back up, paging forward several chapters so that it wouldn't be obvious that I'd just sat there like some kind of love-struck lump for the last half hour.

"You decided to watch that one again?"

"Yeah. Your selection sucks. It's heavy on blood and violence and light on anything redeeming." *Kind of like you.*

"You're lying."

"Why? Are you running one of the lie-detection effects that Jace told me about?"

"No. I can just tell. I guess I just know you too well..."

"I call BS. You don't remember our time together any more than I remember it. You're just screwing with my head."

Kyle sighed. "You're right, I don't remember you—I barely remember Jace—but that doesn't mean I don't still have journals from our time together. I've memorized every passage that includes your name and I read back through them on a regular basis just in case I've forgotten something."

"Wow, that doesn't sound at all stalkerish."

Kyle's smile was sad and more than a little tired. "I know. I've spent more hours than you can imagine wondering if I'm starting the slide into psychosis. I've told myself at least a million times that I'm wasting time that would be better spent in other pursuits, but I can't seem to stop."

"Why?"

The question should have come out dripping with sarcasm. I should have been running away, taking my chances with Fenrir rather than sitting there listening to the guy who was the very definition of a bad ex-boyfriend, but I wasn't. I was genuinely curious.

"Every bit of logic and intellect tells me that I'm on the right course, that this is my best chance to make a lasting difference to the endless violence of our kind, to the pointless cycle of death and rebirth. I know that I'm better off by myself, that I'm more focused on my research now than I ever was before I was wiped clean, but when I read my older journals I can't help but doubt myself."

"Doubt yourself how?"

"I seemed so happy back then. There was a time when I thought that you'd doctored my journals, that you'd gone in and altered them so that I would spend the rest of this incarnation longing for something I couldn't have."

"I would never do that!"

This smile was less sad. It had something to it that somehow felt right. I would have said that this was the kind of smile that the old Kyle used to give me, but there wasn't any way I would have known that.

"You're so quick to assume that this version of you is just like the last version of you."

"Isn't it?"

"It seems like it. The version of you I've read about in my journals would never have done something so vindictive, but of course I had to suspect that you'd edited the journals in such a way as to make me think that you were incapable of editing them."

"Do you ever get lost inside there? It sounds like your head is a pretty twisty, dark place."

"No, not yet, but I suppose there is a first time for everything."

"So what's the verdict?"

"I'm still forming one, but so far it appears that the current you is very much like the you that was the focus of so much of my writing."

"That scares you, doesn't it?"

"Yes. It does indeed. It means that my journals are probably accurate, that the stranger who wrote about you isn't a fabrication, he was just a different version of me, one who was less driven but much happier than this version."

"It sounds like you've got some thinking ahead of you."

That earned me another smile and this one was even more natural than the first.

"I've made a meal. Would you like to come upstairs and eat?"

I very nearly said yes. The last meal was fast becoming a distant memory, and I was only going to get hungrier with each passing hour. As tempting as that was, I wasn't ready to just let him sweep everything under the rug.

"Why did you lie to me earlier?"

"Because I thought I could get away with it."

"That's not what I meant and you know it."

Kyle rubbed his eyes and I remembered for the first time that it had only been a few hours before that he'd been lying on the floor with a broken arm.

"It's a complicated explanation, Selene. As much as I wish I could just tell you everything, there are reasons for my secrecy. Earlier I strayed too close to something that would be safer for you not to know about. When I realized what I'd done, I tried to throw you off the scent. I'm a practiced liar, I should have been successful, but somehow you were able to see through me."

"Is that really such a surprise? You just finished catching me in a lie…"

"Yes, but I have the advantage of my journals. You shouldn't be able to read me this well, not after such a short acquaintance."

"Well, I guess I'm full of even more surprises than you realized."

"Yes. You are indeed."

Chapter 10

The meal was once again simple, but tasty. This time it was homemade tortillas wrapped around a combination of colorful vegetables that had been smothered in lime juice. The biggest shock though was the vase of red roses that were so dark the color was almost three-dimensional.

I stopped breathing for a second when I saw them. Kyle turned back towards me with a shy expression on his face.

"They aren't very aromatic, but they are beautiful. It's a strain called Black Jade—it seemed like something you would like. You always loved flowers."

"You've got a rose bush downstairs in the garden?"

"Several. You couldn't see it from the doorway, but nearly five percent of the usable space downstairs is dedicated to roses."

"Why?"

"Why would I waste space that could have been used to grow more food on something that serves no useful purpose?"

"Yes, that exactly?"

"My original plan didn't include roses or computers. My original plan had me sequestered away down here for decades without any contact with the outside world. I thought that I would be more productive that way and I knew I would be safer."

"So what happened?"

"I got lonely."

I nearly laughed. It was the last thing I'd expected to hear out of Kyle, the man who'd admitted to trading my life away for a few more years of undisturbed research, but there was an earnestness to his manner that told me he was entirely serious.

"You asked earlier why more of our kind didn't hunker down behind powerful wards and wait for the other pantheons to kill each other off. My answer wasn't a lie, but it wasn't the full truth. There is a lot more to the question than I let on.

"Some of us don't isolate ourselves because we want to interact with mortals—because we crave the worship of lesser beings. Others don't go to ground because we're uncomfortable with the idea of shifting over to a completely defensive strategy where it's only a matter of time before someone comes along with a big enough hammer to bring our wards down.

"That's all true, but there's one more piece. We aren't meant to be alone, Selene. There have been rumors for centuries, but I dismissed them. I thought I could endure the isolation, but it turned out that I couldn't."

"You've been making trips out of the bunker for supplies and equipment."

Kyle nodded. "Yes. I tried to tell myself that it was just a matter of upgrading my capabilities. The video feeds and computers have been a tremendous boon, but the truth was that I was just too lonely not to leave this place."

"That's how Mephistoles found you."

"Yes. I thought that I was leaving my bunker at random times, but he'd tracked me down and detected a pattern to my trips. He was waiting for me at the grocery store and it took everything I had to get away with my life. My next trip out was more than a year later and I never went back to that particular town, but there was a message waiting for me on a billboard when I finally did go back to civilization again."

My mind was spinning in shock. I felt so stupid. Of course Kyle had left. There wasn't any other way for him to have agreed not to interfere with Mephistoles' hunt of Kat and I back when my last incarnation ended.

Kyle waited as though hoping that I would say something, but eventually the silence grew to the point where he continued.

"I reached out to him by solving a riddle that only an Awakened could have, and he told me that he was closing in on my position."

I wanted to pick up the flowers and throw them at him—vase and all. "You're so high and mighty, but the truth is that you didn't exchange my last incarnation for a few extra decades of uninterrupted research. You could have easily had that if you'd just stayed hidden underground like you originally planned."

Kyle reached toward me as though trying to comfort me, but I slapped his hands away. If it had been Jace—even if we'd been fighting—I would have let him hold me, but Kyle hadn't earned that right.

"No, don't touch me. You traded my life in, traded twenty years of happiness that I could have had with Jace so that you could have a high-speed internet connection and a big-screen TV."

I turned to run away, but Kyle grabbed my arm and this time there wasn't anything comforting about the gesture. He was amped and the pressure of his hand on my arm was just this side of painful.

"You don't get to run away from me yet, Selene. Once I've finished telling you everything you can run away if that is still what you want to do, but until then you *will* hear me out."

"Why, what else could you possibly tell me?"

Kyle didn't answer. He pulled on my arm, marching me down the stairs until we were standing outside of the level that I hadn't been able to enter. It was only a few seconds' work for Kyle to rekey the ward and then he pushed the door fully open and pulled me into what I could only assume was his research lab.

The walls were covered in chalkboards full of cramped writing that formed a complicated array of equations. One corner of the room was nothing more than a ten foot square chunk of bare concrete enclosed by the shimmering field of an active ward. There wasn't anything but a table inside of the ward, so I could only assume that was his testing area, the place where he performed experiments that might otherwise destroy the contents of the room.

Kyle let go of me and unsheathed his sword. For one terrifying moment I thought he was going to attack me, but instead he reversed the sword and offered it to me hilt first.

"Go ahead, take it."

"Are you really that stupid? Only a complete idiot would hand me a sharp object after manhandling me down all those flights of stairs."

"You're not going to stab me."

"It sounds awfully tempting right about now…"

Kyle just shook his head. "If you were going to attack me you would have done it already. Take the sword and then work the most powerful effect you know how."

I gingerly wrapped my hand around the silver and leather handle, and then nearly dropped the sword when Kyle stepped back and I had to support its entire weight on my own. It was a lot heavier than I expected it to be.

There was enough residual anger still floating around inside me that it was a simple matter to amp my strength up to six times normal. It wasn't the most powerful effect that I knew, but it fit my circumstances the best. I waved the sword around a couple of times, enjoying the fact that it now felt like it weighed no more than a couple of ounces, and then shrugged.

"It's shiny. So what?"

"Can you feel the difference?"

I started to tell him that there wasn't any difference, but before I could get the words out I realized he was right. It was hard to describe. The closest I could come was to say that the imaginary hole in my forehead, the one where my memories streamed out to power my effects, felt...smaller than it should have.

I grabbed the sword with both hands so that I wouldn't drop it, and then canceled the strength amp as I explored the crystalline vista of my memories. I'd used my ability a lot recently so it took me a second to catalogue all of the missing bits and pieces inside of my head.

It made me want to be sick. Ever since I'd nearly lost myself inside of my own head back when I'd first awakened, I'd been purposefully trying not to examine my past too carefully. Now that I was delving deep in an effort to identify all of the missing pieces there wasn't any way to avoid coming to terms with how much I'd traded away in just the last few days.

Five minutes here, ten minutes there, it was starting to add up. Big parts of Ari's fifth birthday party were gone, as was part of a trip to the state fair when I was ten.

The glittering plain inside my head where my memories were stored these days was bigger than it had been—I'd still been creating memories faster than I'd been consuming them—but that was cold comfort. I'd been creating memories of being pursued by Mephistoles and being locked up by Kyle. A million years of those memories could never be as important to me as the memories I'd already lost.

"So much…I've already lost so much."

My knees started to buckle, but Kyle made it to my side before I hit the ground. He wrapped his arms around me, easily bearing my weight over to a utilitarian metal chair as his sword clattered against the floor.

"I know it's hard, Selene, but you have to remember that the alternative was death. This world we live in is more unforgiving than the one you grew up in. If you hadn't used your abilities Fenrir would have killed you before I could make it there to help you. You sacrificed a few memories to save the rest."

"I know, but what happens in ten years or a hundred years? How am I going to feel when I've sacrificed everything that makes me who I am today and all that's left of me is something that I wouldn't recognize?"

"I don't know, Selene. That's the hardest part of being like us. All you can do is try to make sure that you sacrifice your memories in the service of something you believe in, that you write down the things that are the most important to you and resolve never to go back on them."

Something about what he'd just said pulled me back from the edge, made me think that there was a solution to the problem that was over-whelming me.

"You don't just mean journaling my experiences, do you?"

"No. I mean recording rules that you are resolved never to break. I mean listing the things that make you who you are, the lines that you can't cross without becoming someone else altogether."

"What are your rules?"

The question popped out of my mouth before I'd had a chance to really think about what I was asking. I'd just asked for the keys to his soul.

For a second I thought he wasn't going to answer me, but he took a deep breath and then nodded. "I won't tell you all of them, but I can share a few of them. You've probably already guessed some of them. I chose to stand outside of the normal fighting between the pantheons. I decided that I was always going to choose the course that would let me make the greatest long-term contribution to our people, and I swore that I would never again help out my brother."

I jumped back to my feet, breaking his hold around my arms. "That's it? Five or six hundred years of life and all you have to show for it is a bucket list to make sure that you bow out of every possible fight while carrying around a grudge the size of Antarctica?"

Kyle grabbed the chair I'd just been sitting on and threw it across the room with enough force that I half expected it to put a hole in the concrete wall.

"You have no idea what I've been through! You have no right to judge me—you're like a petulant child throwing a fit because you've just been told that the clouds will never rain down money and lollipops!"

"Then stop lecturing me and just *tell* me what's going on. You're right, I don't know very much about how the world works for us Awakened, but I know that Jace is a good person. I can feel it, just like I can feel that you're not supposed to be the villain of this piece.

"For some reason you're determined to do everything possible to make me hate you, but I don't think that's what you really want. I think deep down inside you want to be the good guy, you just don't remember how."

I'd short-circuited his rage once before, but I wasn't expecting to do it again. He went from incensed to calm instantly.

"Who are you?"

"What are you talking about?"

He walked over to the chair he'd just thrown across the room and picked it up. I felt him work a strength amp and then he straightened out the chair and turned back to me.

"You claim to be Selene, but it's like I'm living inside of one of my journals again. The things you are saying are the same things you said to me right after my wipe. They are the things the old you would have said. It's like you never died, like you just dropped off the grid and now are back pretending like you're some innocent seventeen-year-old."

There was such an element of longing in his voice that I couldn't maintain my anger either. "I'm sorry, but she's gone. I'm exactly what I claim to be."

Kyle extended his hand towards his sword and it zipped through the air as though on wires. He inspected the edge and then resheathed it without looking back up at me.

"I'm sorry about your sword—I hope I didn't damage it."

He gave me a bitter smile. "It's the next best thing to indestructible. Think nothing of it—I only wish that I'd managed to unlock its secrets enough to armor my soul with the same material. Did our fight at least distract you from the memories you've lost?"

It had, but before I could tell him as much, I realized what he'd been trying to tell me by giving me his sword. I could feel the block of memories that I'd lost when I'd amped my strength a few seconds before. The gap was just as painful as the rest of the spots where I'd lost part of who and what I was, but it was shorter than I'd been expecting.

"That's what Mephistoles was so worried about. He recognized the sword and knew it was capable of making it so you didn't have to burn as many memories. How does it work?"

Kyle laughed, and the sound was part bitter and part boisterous. "And you instantly divine the heart of the matter. If I knew that I wouldn't still be locked away inside this bunker, I would have already set forth to unite every pantheon under my rule."

"You don't know—you must have theories though…"

"Some. I'm confident that I know what it does, I'm just not sure how it does it. Jace apparently told you about the fae. Did he tell you how they grow?"

"Yeah—oh, I see. It's the 'wasted' memories from effects. Your sword eliminates the waste that is otherwise a natural part of every effect."

"Yes. I haven't done any experiments to confirm that, but Excalibur is a known quantity in that regard. The fae by and large despise this particular artifact. They fear a world where every Awakened wields a similar weapon."

"I can understand why. That would mean there would never be another fae born—it would mean that most of them would never grow any stronger. They would be consigned to an existence where they could never change."

Kyle shrugged. "I'm not convinced that would be an entirely bad thing. For thousands of years we believed that we had a symbiotic relationship with the fae, believed that they thrived off of something that we couldn't use, but it was a lie all along. They are parasites pure and simple."

I thought of Bethany, of her loyalty to the version of me that had created her, and I shook my head. "They didn't ask to be created; they didn't choose to be parasites. Most of them are doing the best they can with the hand that they were dealt."

"The same thing is true of any parasite, Selene. The common cold virus doesn't desire to do us harm, but that doesn't stop it from infecting every host it can find."

"That's where you're wrong, Kyle. The fae can be helpful. They can offer value in exchange for the memories they need from us. Maybe the exchange rate won't be what they are used to, but then again maybe it will."

"You would sacrifice memories that you don't have to sacrifice in exchange for some service? You who was just sobbing over the hours you've already lost?"

I met his gaze without flinching. "Yes, for the right price. If doing so saved someone I cared about then I'd do it in a heartbeat. Even if every Awakened were instantly equipped with an...artifact...like Excalibur that wouldn't mean the end of everything for the fae. There would still be room for all of us."

"I didn't expect you to refute my argument using the language of cold commerce."

"Commerce doesn't have to be cold, Kyle. Just because you're making a trade with someone doesn't mean you don't care about them."

"I detest people who use sentiment to change the terms of an agreement to suit them at the expense of the other party."

"Even if I give you that point, a trade between two people who feel...sentiment...towards each other can still be mutually beneficial."

Kyle started to respond and then stopped. Apparently I'd given him more to chew on than he'd been expecting. I looked at the sword—once again hanging at his waist—and some of the pieces that had been bothering me finally snapped into place.

"That's why Fenrir hasn't ever come after you before now. There wasn't any upside to a fight between the two of you. He knew you had the sword, which meant he wouldn't be able to absorb any of the memories from your attacks."

"Yes, exactly. As things stand right now—even after having absorbed my first two wards—he's come out worse off than he started. He's only continued the assault on my defenses because he rules primarily through fear. If he were to let Awakened or other fae challenge him without consequence he'd soon be overwhelmed with challenges."

"This is about more than just your sword. I would have eventually pieced all of that together just from your last conversation with Mephistoles and Fenrir."

"Indeed. There are plenty of fae who would love to see me dead and Excalibur tossed into the deepest part of the ocean, but that is nothing compared to my true purpose."

I opened my mouth to ask him what he meant, and then it hit me like a bolt of lightning.

"You're trying to create more artifacts. You're trying to create more swords like Excalibur. Oh, my gosh. How could I not see this before now? The field that bends time—that's not something you're actively maintaining—not while you're asleep. You've succeeded, you've figured out how to create artifacts!"

Kyle shook his head. "No. I wish I could confirm your hypothesis, but the truth is that I'm still missing something. The pantheon that lived above us—I've taken to calling them the lost pantheon—succeeded. They left a single artifact behind them and a dozen prototypes that showed their early efforts, but even that hasn't been enough.

"Completed artifacts are incredibly self-contained. I can't just open up Excalibur and snap some pictures to use as a blueprint for my own efforts. There are tests that can be run, but they don't tell me as much as I've been able to learn from the partially-completed prototypes."

"I don't understand. You have all of those prototypes from the lost pantheon. What's the problem?"

"The problem is that they seem to have made some kind of dramatic breakthrough between their last prototype and their artifact. It was something wildly different than their earlier efforts, something I haven't stumbled upon yet."

"So it's all been for nothing then?"

That earned me a proud smile, and Kyle pointed to an egg-shaped metal sphere that was roughly as big as my fist.

"Not all for nothing. I managed to create this. It's not an artifact—it doesn't power itself like a real artifact would—but it does have its uses."

"That's what bends time, isn't it?"

"Yes. Right now it doubles the flow of time here inside of the bunker, which is a huge advantage."

I walked over so I could get a better look at it. The metal had an iridescent sheen that was unlike anything I'd ever seen, but other than that it was unremarkable. It was amazing to think that such a small, innocuous device was responsible for not only speeding up the flow of time over such a large area, but also for figuring out where to end the field so that everything around it didn't crumble as a result of being subject to two different aging speeds.

"So you effectively bought yourself twice as long in which to finish up your research. That was brilliant!"

"Yes, but that's not even the best part. The best part is that the power draw that my device needs to run is only about an eighth of a day's worth of baseline memories for each day that passes outside in the normal world."

"So you're gaining memories faster than everyone else."

"Exactly. It's not a huge number, but it still amounts to a significant advantage over the competition, so to speak, and it uses almost nothing in the way of emotional strength, so it means that we can hit Fenrir twice as often as he expects us to."

A huge grin forced its way out onto my face, but it crumbled away just as fast as it had appeared.

"Not us. You. I'm worse than useless."

"That doesn't have to be the case forever, Selene. I could teach you at least a few basic attacks. Between that and the fact that you already know how to create a time amp, there's every reason to think you could help put the hurt on Fenrir."

"You would do that?"

I wanted to cry. Kyle had already offered me my freedom, and it seemed like he really was legitimately willing to let me leave. The only thing keeping me here now was Fenrir. That meant I was free to hunger after something else. It turned out that what I wanted was more knowledge. I didn't agree with a lot of Kyle's views, but he had one thing completely correct. Knowledge was power, and right now I needed power in a bad way.

Fenrir wasn't just a threat to me, he was a threat to everyone else I cared about. If I was going to stop him then I needed to know how to fight. If Kyle would teach me then I would be more than happy to help take the fight to Fenrir, and I wouldn't stop until he was dead for good.

He would be good practice for when I went after Mephistoles.

Unaware of the direction my thoughts had taken, Kyle nodded. "I would. I want two promises out of you though."

I felt my enthusiasm start to melt away. "What are they?"

"The first one is that you won't use any of the things I'm teaching you against me as long as you're my guest here in the bunker."

Talk about the world's biggest shock. I'd been expecting something overreaching like a promise to *never* use anything I learned against him.

It was like he was reading my mind. "There isn't any good reason to ask for more than that, Selene. We both know that you wouldn't honor your promise if breaking it was required to save my brother."

I wasn't surprised at the bitterness in Kyle's voice when he mentioned Jace. What was surprising was the fact that there was less bitterness there than I'd expected.

"Fine, I can agree to that. What's your second condition?"

"You never breathe a word to anyone about what I've just told you. Not even Jace can know that I've made so much progress when it comes to creating my own artifact."

"I'm not particularly keen to start keeping secrets from Jace and Kat, Kyle. I already have too many secrets in my life just from keeping all of this from my dad and sister."

"I wouldn't ask this of you if I didn't have a good reason, Selene."

"Fine, what's the reason? If you want me to start keeping secrets for you then convince me."

"Every single person who's ever created an artifact died within weeks of it becoming common knowledge."

I shrugged. "That's hardly surprising. You said it yourself, you want to use your knowledge to enslave the rest of us. That's the kind of thing that is bound to make multiple pantheons rise up and try to kill whoever is gunning for the top spot."

Kyle looked like he wished he could go back and just not tell me about his research. "That's just it, Selene. I've managed to get my hands on some journals that everyone thought had been destroyed. I'm not so sure that it was other Awakened who took those researchers down. It's starting to look like the fae—not just one court, but both courts working together—killed them."

"I thought the courts hated each other too much to ever work together."

"Yeah, that's what they want us to think."

Chapter 11

After Kyle's conspiracy theories regarding the Seelie and Unseelie Courts, I wasn't sure what to think. He'd already admitted that extended isolation wasn't good for our kind. Maybe this was all just the delusion of someone who was already three steps too far down the road to crazy town.

I stood there in silence for several seconds as I tried to think through the ramifications of what he was asking me to promise. I considered just lying, but Kyle was uncannily good when it came to reading me. He would probably know if I was less than honest—and then refuse to teach me what I needed to know. Besides, it wasn't in my nature to lie.

In the end, I couldn't come up with a good reason not to promise to keep his secret, so I agreed. Kyle searched my eyes for several seconds before nodding. He walked over to the warded area and rekeyed it so that I could enter.

It turned out that I'd been right in thinking that he used that section for experiments that were too dangerous to perform out in the open. I just hadn't realized that I was going to end up as one of those dangerous experiments.

Kyle once again took me by surprise. I'd expected him to be a grouchy, short-tempered teacher, but he was exactly the opposite of that. He was patient and calm. He'd claimed several times that his true calling was research, but if that was the case all I could figure was that he was hell on wheels behind a microscope because he was an incredible instructor.

Of course it probably helped that I once again picked up the effect he was trying to teach me in record time. I now had a name for the attack that Kat had been using on Fenrir when we'd been running away with Ari. Kyle called it a sun lance, which was way better than calling it a sun beam. I hadn't actually stooped so low as to call Kat's most powerful weapon that—even inside the privacy of my own mind—but it had been tempting a couple of times.

Sun lance was a much tougher, deadlier sounding name. Hopefully it would stick for me so I could avoid pissing Kat off by using the wrong name. The thought of her getting all indignant made me smile.

It was odd that I could be such good friends with people who were so different. Kat was a mind-blowing combination of fear and in-your-face spitfire, while Jace was relaxed—almost passive—until someone threatened us, or we were kissing. Once either of those things happened, he was even more intense than Kat.

Kyle on the other hand was like a mirror image of Jace. He had the shortest temper of anyone I'd ever met, but once you peeled the surface layers back he was shockingly gentle.

That realization made me wonder what it would be like to kiss Kyle, which caused me to instantly blush. Luckily for once Kyle didn't seem to be able to read my mind. I forced all thoughts of kissing—Jace or Kyle either one—out of my mind, and got back to learning the proper way to manifest a sun lance.

I was starting to realize just how many levels of understanding went into crafting an effect. Kyle initially taught me to manifest a sun lance by dwelling on feelings of heat and light until I felt like I was going to burst into flames, and then directing that feeling outward until a golden beam shot out from my hand and spent itself against the shimmering wall of Kyle's wards.

When I demonstrated mastery of that way of doing things, Kyle began adding refinements to my style. It was just like what I'd noticed the first time I'd amped myself after waking up in Kyle's bed. Apparently you could brute-force nearly any effect, but the more you understood about what went into the effect—in this case the way that waves and particles functioned—the more powerful you could make it.

There was an obvious lesson there, but it also felt like there was another, more subtle realization waiting for me if I could just reach out and grab it. It was an unsettling sensation, the kind of thing that normally would have stayed with me like a splinter in the back of my mind, but this time around my efforts to master the sun lance were sufficient to distract me from the feeling.

After a little more than an hour I finally managed to master the effect at what Kyle figured was about twice the strength I'd started out with.

"I'm not sure I'll ever manage to be anything more than an irritant to someone like Fenrir."

Kyle shook his head. "You're doing an amazing job picking this up. Most Awakened would still be trying to get a handle on the regular-strength effect, and you've taken things to the next level already. A double-strength sun lance isn't going to be enough to put Fenrir down, but he'll know he's been hit by it."

"So what comes next?"

Kyle walked over to one of the large free-standing cabinets that surrounded the metal-working equipment in the center of the room, and pulled out a heavy-looking sword.

"Under other circumstances I would probably keep working with you until you managed a triple-strength lance, but I think we'd be better off taking a trip out to the third ward and doing as much damage as we can to Fenrir before his friends show up."

My throat went instantly dry. "Do you really think that I'm ready?"

"You'll be just fine. Your emotional reserves are probably a little on the low side, but you should still have enough to amp yourself up to four or five times normal speed and still have enough left over to hit Fenrir with two or three lances. The key thing is to stay as close to the ward as possible. Step across, hit him with a lance, and then step back to the other side where you are safe before he can get close enough to hurt you."

Kyle handed me the sword and I was surprised at how much heavier it was than Excalibur. I was able to lift it with two hands, but only just.

"I don't have a sheath for that one, so you'll have to carry it like that, but you won't have any problems wielding it once you're amped up."

"All the strength in the world isn't going to help me given that I don't know the first thing about using one of these things."

"Yeah, we'll get into the proper way to swing a sword before the next time we go after Fenrir and company. I don't expect you to need it, but if nothing else get it between you and Fenrir and let the force of his charge push you back through the ward."

"Okay. Let's go do this before I lose my nerve and run away with my tail between my legs."

Kyle gave me a funny look. "You're many things, Selene Jenkins, but you're not a coward. Just remember that we have to go through Fenrir before you'll be able to go help rescue your dad."

I was shocked at the wave of warmth that crashed through me in response to Kyle's praise. Somehow the fact that the praise had come from Kyle made it more valid, more real than if it had come from anyone else.

I couldn't manage a verbal response after that. I just nodded and gestured for Kyle to lead the way. I half expected him to rekey the ward to his workshop as we left, but he didn't. It was another sign that he trusted me more than I would have if our positions had been reversed.

We stopped off to confirm that Fenrir hadn't managed to bring down the third ward yet. Kyle said it was nothing more than a formality, that he would be able to sense the third ward as soon as we'd stepped across the boundary of the fourth ward, but I wasn't going to complain about a few extra precautions. The last thing I wanted was for Fenrir to take us by surprise out in the middle of the Lost City when we were too far away from Kyle's wards to disengage at will.

Kyle stopped at the top of the stairs to confirm that his new shoes were properly laced, and then inspected my shoes. They were much the worse for the wear as a result of my earlier sprint up the stairs, but he seemed to think that they would do the job still.

"When we get out to the third ward we need to drift away from each other. We need to make sure that there's enough space between us that Fenrir can't come after both of us at the same time."

"Okay, I'll just pretend that I don't like you. That shouldn't be too hard."

It was the wrong thing to say just before we headed off for battle, and I knew it as soon as the words left my mouth. I expected Kyle to get offended, but he just rolled his eyes.

"I'd say that I don't remember you being this sarcastic, but that's not the case—I just don't remember you."

Now it was my turn to roll my eyes. "Touché. So how do you expect this to go down?"

"Fenrir will have to choose one of us as his primary target. It could go either way, but I suspect he's going to figure that you aren't as much of a threat as I am. If that's the case he'll come after me and I'll do my best to cut him up without letting him get his teeth on me."

"Which means I can just stand back and hit him with sun lances until I don't have any emotional reserves left."

"Yeah. The next fight will be more interesting. Fenrir will know that you're capable of hurting him, so he might charge you in the hopes of eliminating you right off the bat."

"Oh, goody."

Kyle opened up the door to the bunker and we headed out into the abandoned city. I made a note to ask Kyle to teach me how to create a floating ball of light, but knew better than to say anything while we were outside of the security of the bunker. It was better if Fenrir didn't know Kyle was actively teaching me new effects until I hit him with my first sun lance.

A few minutes later we arrived at the third ward. I recognized one of the hallways a dozen yards before the ward and fixed a scowl on my face a few seconds before Fenrir was able to see us. I put more than a dozen yards between Kyle and I by the time I finally stopped in front of the ward.

"Back so soon, Kyle? I'm surprised. I expected you to spend hours still licking your wounds after our last encounter."

"Indeed I am. I'd say that I came back to offer to let you walk away now before you lose even more of your strength, but we both know I can't go back on my word."

"No more than I can, but you're pursuing a fool's errand. I've absorbed enough energy from your ward to nearly replace everything you took away from me in our last clash."

"I guess I'll just have to work harder this time."

I felt Kyle amp himself up with a warm rush that reminded me of the way I felt when my anger was roaring along at full tilt. He'd caught me nearly as much by surprise as he had Fenrir, but when I reached for my anger it was more than happy to crash into the front of my mind.

The sight of Kyle flickering across the ward, unsupported nearly brought me to panic. I reached out to amp my system and once again reached for more than I would have if I'd taken the time to think about what I was doing.

Luckily something clicked again for me and the effects that clicked into place were the more extensive set of changes that I'd managed when I'd been trying to run away from Kyle. I shifted my now-feather-light sword into my right hand and stepped across the ward as Kyle dodged to one side to avoid Fenrir's charge.

It was obvious that Fenrir didn't expect the attack to score; he was just trying to push Kyle out where it would be harder to retreat away from the ward if Kyle got into trouble.

Fenrir spun around with a speed that should have been impossible in something so big, and then arrowed toward Kyle, but Kyle once again spun away. Fenrir had brushed him with a massive shoulder, and the force of the blow would have shattered the bones of someone operating under a less extreme set of augmentations, but Kyle managed to get a long slash of his own in and Fenrir was bleeding as he whipped around to take another pass.

I took a deep breath, grimacing at the way the thick, viscous air refused to fill my lungs, and then I reached down deep for the heat and light I'd only just mastered.

The sun lance shot out of my hand and hit exactly where I'd wanted it to strike. The blow landed right in the deepest part of the cut Kyle had just made on Fenrir's flank, and staggered the big wolf. It couldn't have come at a better time; it let Kyle slide out of the way of Fenrir's next attack and this time his sword licked out and took Fenrir across the back left leg.

It was the kind of blow that I thought should have taken the leg off completely, but some unnatural vitality turned the blow enough that Fenrir got to keep the limb. It was still a big win for us though because I could already tell that Fenrir had lost some of his mobility.

The big wolf hopped to the side, trying to knock Kyle over with his shoulder. He succeeded to a degree, throwing Kyle into a nearby wall, but Kyle bounced off the wall like he was made out of rubber and his sword took Fenrir across the nose again at the same time that I cut loose with another superheated bar of golden light.

This time I didn't manage to catch Fenrir completely off guard and my beam only carved into his flesh for a second before he slid out of the way and the last half of my attack wasted itself against the rock wall a few yards away from Kyle.

I was astonished at just how much damage I'd done to the wall. My sun lance had carved a trench into the stone nearly a foot deep and two feet long, but all it had managed to do to Fenrir was burn away a fist-sized divot out of his hip.

I was still processing the results of my last attack when Fenrir spun around and charged towards me with a speed that dwarfed anything I'd ever seen out of him before. It didn't seem fair that he could both turn faster than either of us and be so much faster in a straight line.

The abrupt change in tactics paralyzed me for a fraction of a heartbeat. I raised my sword, instinctively trying to get *something* between me and the two or three tons of charging dire wolf, and then remembered Kyle's order to jump back through to the other side of the ward.

Just as I started to take my first step, Fenrir put on the brakes and turned so he could snap at Kyle. My heart jumped up into my throat. Kyle had committed himself too heavily. He'd been so worried about catching Fenrir before the wolf could make it to me that he'd come in too fast.

Fenrir's jaws snapped shut and I thought for a second that the fight was over, but Kyle threw himself over top of Fenrir, spinning like a corkscrew, his sword flashing as it sliced into Fenrir's neck.

It was a masterful display of acrobatics and strength, but it was going to fail. Kyle hadn't had any other options open to him, but the cut to Fenrir's neck hadn't been fatal and the wolf was already whipping around to make sure he would be able to sink his teeth into Kyle before Kyle could land and change direction again.

Kyle seemed to be moving in slow motion. Our eyes met and it was obvious that he knew he'd failed. He opened his mouth, probably to tell me to get back behind the ward, but I didn't give him a chance to get the words out.

I once again reached down for the heat and light I needed to generate another sun lance, but this time there was something different about my effort. The rage that had served me so well up until now was a shadowy, brittle thing. There wasn't enough of the emotion left to fuel the effect I needed, so I reached out and instead found an all-consuming happiness waiting for me.

I wasn't happy that Kyle was about to die, but there was something about knowing another person was willing to sacrifice themselves for me that demanded my gratitude and it was a very short trip from gratitude to happiness.

I grabbed hold of every ounce of emotion left to me, both happiness and rage, and forged it into heat that exceeded anything I'd ever felt before. The earlier sun lance—the one that had felt like an unquenchable bonfire—was nothing more than a candle in comparison to the supernova of destruction that burst out of my right hand.

The beam of light crashed into Fenrir with the weight of a wrecking ball and I realized that I'd just consumed my first peak memory. I couldn't have said for sure what it was. The missing piece was bigger than I'd expected, like it had consumed everything that gave the peak memory context. It seemed to have taken place at an amusement park, so maybe it had been my first rollercoaster ride.

I felt a pang of loss once again at having traded away part of what made me the person I was, but even that was drowned out by amazement at the sheer amount of damage I'd managed to inflict on Fenrir.

My sun lance didn't just throw him into the nearest wall, it also vaporized a four-foot chunk of flesh and bone out of his shoulder. For the first time I could see fear in Fenrir's eyes.

I started to smile and then something, maybe the sound of wings, brought me around to my right. My sword was out of position, and the creature flying toward me was much too close, but I had no other choice but to at least try to get my weapon into play.

The fae was only slightly bigger than a monkey, but its tattered, bat-like wings, and scaly skin made my skin crawl. The two-inch knife-like claws on the end of its fingers and toes were flexing in anticipation, and it was already within inches of my unprotected flesh.

There was another fae behind it, this one in the shape of a dark horse that walked on claw-tipped fists, but I knew I was going to be dead before the horse made it close enough to be a threat. Fenrir had outsmarted us. He'd lured us out and then kept us occupied for long enough that the other Unseelie fae had been able to get within striking range.

I opened my mouth to scream my defiance at the snake monkey that was about to kill me, and then a ball of crackling darkness hit the smallest fae, knocking it away from me at the last second.

"Get back behind the ward!"

Kyle's yell broke the shocked immobility that I'd been laboring under, and I turned just in time to see Fenrir lunge back towards him. I tried to warn him, but Fenrir—even with a smoking hole in his shoulder—was just too fast. Kyle started turning, but it was too late and Fenrir's jaws closed around Kyle's left shoulder.

It was hard to separate out Kyle's scream from mine, but we both went on the offensive. I cut loose with a second peak-memory-powered sun lance and then a split second later, I saw another bar of glowing liquid gold erupt out of the back of Fenrir's neck.

The paired, peak memory attacks had done what no single attack had managed yet. We'd both targeted the same spot on Fenrir's spine, me from the outside, Kyle from inside the dire wolf's throat where his hand was trapped, and we'd managed to kill him.

The sound of the approaching fae from my right drove me back across the ward as my emotional reserves evaporated and my sustained effects all fell away. My sword was almost too heavy for me to lift, but I grabbed on with both hands and pointed it towards the dark horse as I prepared to charge back through the ward.

"No!"

I spun around just in time to see Kyle stumble back across the wards, arm hanging limply at his side, blood streaming from his wound.

Chapter 12

"Heal yourself! You've got to do it now before you lose too much blood!"

I caught him before he could hit the ground, but Kyle looked up at me with glassy, uncomprehending eyes, and I knew it was too late. He was already too far gone, but I didn't want to give up on him. I lowered him the rest of the way to the ground and applied pressure to the spot on the front of his shoulder that seemed to be bleeding the worst, trying to buy him time to come out of shock.

I knew nothing about healing effects, but I still would have tried to do something if I'd had any emotional reserves left. Instead I did the only other thing I could think of that might help. I hauled back and slapped Kyle as hard as I could.

"Don't you dare leave me here by myself!"

Barely visible into the faint illumination of his dying light effect, his eyes started to roll back up into his head, and then he shuddered. I realized in that moment that I'd never seen the full extent of Kyle's will. His body was failing him, his abilities were exhausted, he had to be in unimaginable pain, but he forced himself back from the edge.

The flesh underneath my left hand heated up like the world's worst sunburn at the same time that I felt his power flow outwards like a million electrically charged ants. The jolt of discharging energy did what even the risk of second-degree burns hadn't been able to do, and I reflexively pulled my hand back.

I expected to see blood pouring out of damaged arteries, but the skin was unblemished—even the blood had been burned away.

"You did it!"

Kyle looked up at me and weakly shook his head. "I stopped the blood loss, but I couldn't do anything about the venom."

The effort of healing so much damage finally caught up with him, and this time even Kyle's will wasn't enough to fight off uncon-sciousness. The tiny orb floating above him disappeared at the same instant, leaving us in complete darkness.

A loud crack and the bright discharge of high-voltage electricity brought me around to see the black fae horse thrown more than forty feet through the air. There was a second crack, this time the meaty sound of breaking bones, when the fairy hit the rock wall, and I dared hope for the briefest of seconds that the ward had been strong enough to kill it.

My hope was short-lived. A couple of seconds later the four-legged form started moving around again. The ward hadn't been strong enough to kill it, but based on the way it was moving, it wasn't strong enough to take down our defenses. That was good, it meant that we were safe until Fenrir reformed and came back.

Part of me was hoping that this most recent death would be enough to make even Fenrir too weak to tackle our defenses, but I knew that was just wishful thinking. I needed to get moving, needed to at least get Kyle back behind the fourth ward. I wasn't qualified to judge how much more abuse the third ward could take. It might last for another couple of days, or it might come down the next time any of our attackers pushed up against it. Either way I didn't feel safe with nothing more than it between us and three Unseelie Court fairies who desperately wanted to end our current incarnations.

I checked once again, trying to summon a strong enough emotion to work at least a strength amp, but there just wasn't anything left. I carefully slid my sword through the front of Kyle's belt, sheathed Excalibur at his waist, and then grabbed both his arms and started dragging him across the cold, stone floor as Kyle's ward finally bled off enough energy for it to get dark again.

IMMORTAL

Dragging Kyle was physically the hardest thing I'd ever done. The tiny ridges in the stone that I'd been so impressed with on my first trip through the city were great for providing extra traction, but right then I would have traded them for something slicker, something that would have made it less of a challenge to keep Kyle moving.

As hard as it was physically to pull the better part of two hundred pounds of dead weight across the floor, dealing with the complete lack of light was almost worse. I'd gotten a good look at my surroundings as the discharge from the wards had lit up everything for several hundred yards, but it only took a few seconds for me to start feeling disoriented.

I nearly had a breakdown right then and there. There was an incessant flicker that I kept seeing out of the corner of my eye that caused my skin to crawl and shivers to work their way up and down my spine, but in the end it was the flicker that saved me.

Within a couple of minutes my joints were aching and my muscles were burning, but I was slowing down more because I knew I was wandering around aimlessly than because of the exhaustion pulling at me like a lead weight.

I happened to be looking in exactly the right spot to see the flicker again and finally realized what it was. It was the time-bending effect from Kyle's pseudo-artifact. It wasn't a perfect guide, but I'd watched it on both of the last two trips out of the bunker and it had always formed a kind of shallow 'V' with Kyle at the front.

It made sense, expanding the area of the effect couldn't be cheap from an energy perspective, so he'd created it to expand only in the direction he was moving. That was some-thing I could use.

I stopped pulling and carefully walked around Kyle until I could pick up his feet and pull him a couple of inches back the direction we'd just come from. My sword grated on the stone in a way that set my teeth on edge, but it only took a couple of inches before I saw the flicker again as the time bend expanded out again.

It wasn't much to wager our lives on, but I thought that I could make out a line where the field ended. The darkness inside the field was richer. There was a depth to it that reminded me of velvet or the roses that had been waiting for me on the table at our last meal.

I carefully marked the middle of the field and adjusted our course so that we were traveling towards what I thought was Kyle's bunker. Now that I knew what I was looking for I made better time. It was still brutally hard to continue forward with nothing more than my normal, unamped strength to do the work, but now I could use the erratic jumps of Kyle's field to fine-tune our course as we went.

I started crying when I saw the fourth ward. It was just a faint shimmer in the darkness that didn't give off any usable light, but it told me that I'd at least managed to get us behind the next layer of protection.

I wanted to take it as a sign that we were going to make it safely back to the bunker, but that was still far from guaranteed. We were headed in roughly the right direction, but all it would take was for me to end up going down the wrong hall for us to never find the actual doorway down into the bunker.

It was a journey of several hundred yards, and all it would take to miss the bunker would be for me to be off by a few feet one way or the other at any point along the way.

I started shivering—from cold rather than just from fear—about the time I hit the fifth ward. It took me another dozen yards before I realized what was going on. The Lost City was the same temperature as always, a bit on the cool side, but that wasn't enough to explain the way my body temperature was dropping.

It was Kyle. His hands were like ice and he was sucking the heat out of me at an alarming rate. I was running out of time.

I couldn't have said where I found the strength, but I managed to pick up the pace and it was only a few more minutes before I noticed that the darkness wasn't as fierce as it had been previously.

It was the bunker. With all my freaking out I'd forgotten that Kyle had left the door to the bunker open and the lights from inside were just enough to guide me into the right hallway. Given how hard it had been for me to drag Kyle, I didn't have high hopes for being able to get him down the stairs without killing both of us, but it wasn't like I really had much of a choice. I pulled him inside to the landing at the very top of the stairs and then swung the massive door shut behind us.

I pulled Excalibur out of its sheath and left it and my sword both at the top of the stairs—as exhausted as I was, an extra fifteen pounds might make the difference between success or failure. My hands were useless blocks of wood, but I knew there wasn't time to stop and wait for my body to warm back up now that we were inside the bunker.

I picked Kyle up from behind, wrapping my arms around his chest since my hands weren't functioning, and slowly backed down the flight of stairs to the first level, hoping the entire time that my back wasn't going to give out on me before we at least made it to the couch. Ironically, once we got to the couch I was too exhausted to get him up on it.

I set him down on the floor next to it and forced myself down the stairs at something at least slightly faster than the shambling walk my body kept telling me was the best we could manage. Everything I'd ever heard or read about hypothermia was racing through my head the entire way down to Kyle's bedroom.

Just having my arms around his chest had made them ache—he was that cold. He wasn't even shivering, and I had to assume that everything that was happening right now was because of the poison. It was possible that nothing I could do would make the slightest bit of difference, but I had to at least try. If he was freezing to death from the inside out, then I was going to have to try to warm him up from the outside in and the only blankets I for sure knew about were on his bed.

Less than five minutes later I was back with the heavy comforter from his bed. I draped it across the couch and then lifted him up onto the couch, climbed on top of him, and pulled the comforter over both of us.

It was like hugging a snowman. My hands were already numb and my arms had been aching from the cold, but now it was my entire body pressed up against him and my core temperature was dropping faster than I'd realized it would.

To say that I was shivering would have been a profound understatement. I felt like my body was going to shake itself apart, and I realized that there was a distinct possibility that he was too cold, that he was going to suck all of the heat out of me and kill us both, but I stayed there under the covers with him.

I didn't have any other choice. Without him I was dead anyway, and I was pretty sure that

Jace, Kat, my dad, and Ari would all follow along behind within a matter of days or weeks.

I'd read somewhere that it's a bad idea to let yourself fall asleep when you're extremely cold, that it's just your body's way of shutting down, but I couldn't seem to stop myself. Eventually the cold got to be too much and I closed my eyes.

Chapter 13

I woke up feeling like I was on fire, which didn't make sense because I was perfectly comfortable in every other way. Jace and I fit together like we'd been designed for each other. Lying there with my head resting on his chest, his arms around my waist, felt like perfection. I couldn't remember ever sleeping better than that, which I was pretty sure wasn't usually the way it was supposed to be.

I reached up to run my hand across the stubble along his jaw, and reality finally blew away the cobwebs around my mind. Jace's breathing wasn't right, it was too shallow and quick, and I shouldn't be hot, I should be cold.

No, not Jace, Kyle. Everything came crashing back to me and my eyes popped open. I'd never turned off the lights, so I could see that Kyle was flushed and panting. It seemed impossible that he'd gone from freezing cold to burning hot, but I couldn't argue with what I was feeling.

I threw the blankets off of us and rolled off of him, but I knew that wasn't going to be enough. Any time a fever in an adult reached one hundred and five degrees you risked brain damage. I didn't have a thermometer, but I was pretty sure that Kyle had crashed into the danger zone while I'd still been asleep. Just uncovering him wasn't going to be enough to bring a fever like this down.

I reached for my anger and felt it crash into me with welcome strength. There was plenty to be mad about, everything from my dad being Mephistoles' prisoner to the fact that Kyle might die at any minute, but that was okay, anger was what I needed to save him.

I amped my strength up to three or four times normal and picked Kyle up so that he was hanging across my right shoulder. The trip down to his bedroom took less than sixty seconds and then I was carefully lowering him into his gigantic bathtub.

I checked his pockets, put his wallet on the side of the tub and then turned the cold water on full-force as I let my strength amp lapse. It wasn't going to be enough—the tub was too big, it was going to take forever to fill.

I could feel him radiating heat even from inches away, half an inch of water wasn't going to do the trick. I stood there looking for a solution for several seconds and then I turned and ran back towards the stairs, amping myself back up to triple speed on my way.

I ransacked the kitchen, trying very hard not to rip the cabinet doors off of their hinges as I went. Kyle's refrigerator was older than I was. There was ice in the freezer, but it was just in a pair of white plastic trays. I grabbed them anyway and then snagged a pair of big glass pitchers as I flew back downstairs.

I'd known that the tub was filling up slowly, that I had time still, but part of me had still been worried that I was going to come back and find Kyle drowning. He wasn't, the water was still less than an inch deep, but he was weakly thrashing around, pulling at his shirt like it was burning him.

I set both pitchers down and grabbed his shirt. I only intended on pulling it up out of the way, but it had taken more than its fair share of damage from Fenrir's attack and it tore like tissue paper. I turned the tray over and dumped the ice cubes onto Kyle's chest, hoping that they would buy us enough time for the tub to finish filling up.

The ice cubes from the second tray joined the ones from the first tray, and then I grabbed both pitchers and took them over to the massive sink that took up a significant percentage of the space underneath the eight-foot-tall mirror.

I turned the cold water on in the sink, and then shoved the first pitcher under the stream. As soon as it was halfway full I swapped it out for the second pitcher and then hurried back over to the tub so I could pour the cold water on Kyle, starting at the bottom, soaking his jeans so that the wet material would help regulate his body temperature.

It continued on like that for what felt like forever, but which couldn't have been more than another half hour or so. By the time the water was covering up his ears, the ice cubes had long since melted and I'd realized my next problem—I couldn't just leave Kyle in the water like that or he was going to drown.

I turned the water in the sink off, set the pitchers aside and then bent down to check the temperature of the water. It was cool, but by no means as cold as it had been when it came out of the tap, and if anything Kyle was just as hot as he'd been before I'd put him in the tub.

I slipped out of my shoes and socks, emptied my pockets, and then climbed into the tub with Kyle so that I could hold his head up out of the water. I rested his head on my lap and used my hands to splash water up onto his chest, praying the whole time that his fever would break, and that he'd be okay. I needed him to be the same Kyle he'd been before he'd been injured, needed his help if I was going to get out of this underground prison.

As the water got deeper I debated turning it off, but at the rate he was warming up the water that was already in the tub I knew that wasn't an option. Instead I just pulled him up so that his head was lying against my chest and held him there.

At first I tried to keep him as far away from my body as possible, but the water was just so cold that I eventually pulled him tight against me, desperately trying to steal enough heat from him to keep from going into hypothermia.

It felt like we were in there forever. I eventually shifted us around so that we were over by the drain and as the tub started to fill up too much I let some of the warmer water out while the tap continued to send down a stream of icy cold liquid.

At some point I felt Kyle shift around again. His fevered thrashing had subsided as I'd managed to get him fully immersed in the water, and if not for the slow rise and fall of his chest I would have been worried that he was dead.

"What happened?"

Actually hearing him speak was such a shock that I nearly let his head fall under the water. Mentally cursing myself for being an idiot, I tightened my hold on the edge of the tub with my left hand, and then shifted my right arm lower on the slick, bare skin of his chest so that I could pull him up higher.

"We were fighting Fenrir. He bit you—you healed the damage to your shoulder, but then you said something about poison and passed out. I dragged you through the darkness and by some miracle managed to make it back here to your bunker, but by then your core temperature had dropped dangerously low. I got you warmed up, but then you spiked a fever. I thought for a second that I was going to lose you."

He turned his head toward my voice. For a second I thought he was going to respond, but then I realized that his eyes were still closed. I'd managed to cool him down enough for him to start dreaming—that or maybe he was hallucinating—but he still didn't know where he was.

"Figures that I would get all excited thinking that you were finally coherent and it turns out that you're still off in Never-Never Land. You probably think I'm the old me, the one you let Mephistoles kill."

"I never wanted it to happen that way, Genevieve...couldn't stop him...bluffed him into thinking I could. I figured you'd want it that way...you'd want at least some good to come out of your death."

That was the first time anyone had ever mentioned my old name. Then again, I hadn't exactly been badgering anyone about that particular subject. Maybe I'd been scared to know too much about who I'd been before, scared that it would make it harder to be this version of me if I knew too much about the earlier version, the one that everyone was so excited about.

"Was that my name back in the day?"

"Always your name. I've forgotten nearly everything else over the years and had to relearn it from my journals, but I've never forgotten that."

Kyle still wasn't what I'd call responsive, but him talking had snapped me out of the funk that I'd settled into while trying to keep him from drowning or overheating. I really looked at him for the first time since I'd climbed into the bathtub with him, and the beginnings of desire started to course through me.

He'd never been as big and muscly as Jace, but the cold and fever had taken more out of him than I would have believed possible. He'd lost at least four or five pounds of fat on a frame that hadn't had much more than that on it to start out with.

If it kept up for much longer his body would have to start consuming muscle, but for now it had just chiseled away everything extraneous from his form. His skin was like tissue paper stretched over warm granite muscles. Watching his chest rise and fall made me feel all warm and tingly.

A week ago I would have said that nobody could have triggered such a strong reaction in me. A couple of days ago I would have said that nobody but Jace could create such an instant tidal wave of aching desire inside of me, but it turned out I would have been wrong on both counts.

My arms were getting tired. I shifted Kyle around, trying to take some of his weight off of my right arm, and then I saw the other effect of him having lost so much weight. His pants were riding even lower than they had before Fenrir had gotten his teeth into Kyle. I suddenly realized that all it would take was one wrong move and Kyle's jeans would slide right off his hips.

"Whoa there, girl. You are not going to jump Kyle's bones. Not ever, but especially not when he's unconscious and hallucinating."

Kyle had gone limp again. I shook him, hoping that I'd be able to get him more coherent rather than less.

"Kyle, how do I heal you? Tell me how to bring you back from this."

I would have slapped him again, but the angle was all wrong for that. Luckily something about the sound of my voice brought him at least partially back to me. In someone else the weak movement of his head wouldn't have even been worth commenting on, but given everything he'd been through in the last few hours it was the next best thing to him jumping out of the tub and doing handsprings.

"I can't go back. Some things can't be healed."

"You're hallucinating, Kyle. I don't know what you think is going on, but I need you to snap out of it enough to tell me how to work a healing effect. You remember my name from two or three hundred years ago, please tell me that isn't the only thing left up there."

"Silly...Genevieve. Of course that's not it. I remember your birthday, too. March fourteenth, the same as ours. You were born with snow on the ground. It's all in your journal—on the bottom shelf. Born in the spring, in the mountains with snow all around. Just like now, cold snow...so cold."

I started to shake him again, but then I realized that he wouldn't ever notice, not with the way he was already shivering. Mentally cursing that I'd been too busy drooling over Kyle's awesome bod to realize that his fever had broken, I amped myself enough that I could force him to a sitting position.

As I reached for the tap to shut off the cold water, I brushed up against his arm and realized for the first time how cold he'd gotten. His fever hadn't just broken, he was headed back into hypothermia. I was back exactly where I'd started, only this time he was dripping wet and weakened from running a raging fever for hours which had burned up reserves he hadn't had a chance to replenish because I hadn't even tried to get anything down him.

I struggled to my feet and held Kyle in one arm for a second as I debated options. In the end I just gritted my teeth and slipped his jeans off. There wasn't time to let his boxers drip dry, so I grabbed two towels on my way to the bed.

One towel went on the bed so I could sit him down and dry his chest and back, and then I let him fall back to the bed and soaked up the water from his legs in smooth, quick motions. Thirty seconds later he was lying on the bed with a towel wrapped around his waist to soak up the water still dripping from his underwear.

I grabbed three more towels, two to drape over him and one for me, and then I stripped out of my clothes, trying not to let the fact that my boyfriend's brother was unconscious less than a dozen feet away make me feel self-conscious. I failed miserably, but at least I stopped it from slowing me down.

Even though there wasn't anyone around to see me other than Kyle if I wanted to run around naked, I wrapped my damp towel around my body and headed back up the stairs at a run—I already knew that a couple of dry towels weren't going to be enough to stop Kyle's temperature from crashing.

It took me just over a minute this time to get back downstairs with his comforter, and I begrudged every second, including the ten seconds it took me to pull on one of the clean t-shirts from his dresser drawer, and then I was under the covers with him, wrapping my body around him in an attempt to warm him back up.

Chapter 14

Being under a blanket with Kyle with less than a full change of clothes between the two of us would have tried the resolve of a saint, and I'd recently realized just how far away I was from sainthood. Every time he moved I could feel his muscles rippling against me. My arms, my legs, my stomach, my chest, every single part of me that touched him seemed hyper-aware of the fact that he was nothing more than hard planes covered by warm, perfect skin.

The only thing that saved me was the fact that I knew Jace was waiting faithfully for me, that he'd be hurt if he found out that something had happened between Kyle and me—that and the fact that Kyle was unconscious. Still, it was more than two torturous hours later before I was finally able to untangle myself from Kyle and venture back upstairs. Even then I only stayed away long enough to ransack his pantry and microwave a can of chicken noodle soup. The entire exercise took only minutes, but I spent the entire time worried that I was going to come back down and find that he'd spiked a temperature again—or worse.

Luckily he was still stable when I got back, shivering slightly without my body heat, but still breathing, still alive. Feeding an unconscious person with a spoon was a lot harder than I'd expected it to be. The only thing that saved me was the fact that I had the ability to make myself strong enough to manhandle him as needed. I piled all of the pillows from his gigantic bed against the headboard and pulled him up against them so that he was very nearly in a sitting position and then spooned the broth into his mouth a little bit at a time.

He choked and coughed a little bit at the start, and then his swallowing reflex seemed to take back over and half an hour later the broth was all gone and he was shivering badly enough that I crawled back under the comforter again.

I was emotionally and mentally exhausted, but my body wasn't ready to sleep yet. Luckily, once Kyle's hunky body was out of sight under the covers it was apparently out of mind too. Of course not wrapping myself around him this time probably helped—I wasn't sure I could have taken another round of carnal temptation so soon after the last one, not when I was feeling worn out and shaky with concern over whether or not he was going to survive unscathed.

Instead I suffered through a different kind of temptation. Kyle had mentioned a journal—my journal—and he'd made it sound like he possessed it. I'd spent the first little while after Jace found me wishing that I could do more to distance myself from the shadowy figure of my previous incarnation, but now that I knew what her name—my name—had been, I was intensely curious about what she'd been like.

I must have looked at the bottom row of white, leather-bound journals a million times while I waited for Kyle to warm back up to the point where he wasn't in danger of having his organs spontaneously shut down. There were only twelve of them on the bottom shelf, only twelve books that I'd have to crack open and look at if I wanted to satisfy my suspicion.

I'd never been that kind of girl, the one who snooped around in stuff that wasn't any of her business, but as I lay there with my back to Kyle and temptation just a few yards away I realized that it wasn't that I didn't have some of those tendencies, it was just that I was usually able to distract myself from them.

That wasn't an option this time. I couldn't go work out, I couldn't go cook myself something to eat, I couldn't even go take a cold shower. For all I knew Kyle might spike another fever at any minute, and even if he didn't there was a limit to how long I could leave him before he would start cooling off and shivering again.

I was stuck between staying there touching Kyle's perfect skin without anything to distract me, or looking at the journals. In the end I chose the lesser sin. I padded over to the bookshelves and opened up the book furthest to the right.

Pay dirt. The volume I was holding seemed to switch back and forth between French and English, but it was the one I wanted, the one that I'd been hoping for. I opened up the next book just to confirm that I was right, but I didn't need to see the more masculine handwriting to know that the first book wasn't written by Kyle.

I set both books back on the shelf, bit my lip, and then grabbed my journal and hurried back to the bed. Kyle might end up mad, I might end up regretting ever picking up this particular volume, but I had to know.

Journal Entry
April 3, 1724

Kyle has been after me to practice my English. I tell him it doesn't matter, that I'm still going to sound French, but it turns out he's less worried about my accent than he is about the notes I've been sending him.

Tensions between here and the Continent are running high again and it looks exceedingly bad for a recently elevated count of the realm to be seen receiving notes written in a tongue that most of the royal family has never bothered to learn. So much for the advantages of a classical education.

I tried to convince Kyle to deputize Jace to go in his place, but he's been even less flexible than usual with regards to those kinds of things here in our new home. I truly wish we'd been able to stay in Paris. We had such a good life there, but the four of us simply can't match Nikoli's thugs.

I simply can't do justice to the outrage I feel every time I think about our loss. Despite all our learning, despite the fruits of decades of careful, inspired research, we're still at the mercy of bullies like the Kiev pantheon. The human world has seen a resurgence of civilization over the last few lifetimes, but among our kind, might is still what makes right.

I suppose Kyle is right. We can't afford to risk our position here—not unless we're prepared to journey across the ocean and try to make a life for ourselves there. Jace and Kat are both enamored of the idea, but there is no telling what might await us there. Better the devil we know than a dangerous trip into darkness. Our research is simply too important to risk on some flight of fancy.

We aren't the only pantheon here in England, but Ashwell's group seems content to leave us alone for now as long as we continue to work towards the best interest of the nobility. The royal family is still completely unaware that we are anything more than we claim, but Kyle is right. All it would take is a hint of treason for us to find *royal guardsmen on our doorstep with orders to see us to a prison.*

They couldn't take us anywhere we didn't want to go, of course, but I'm tired of killing humans, and even our kind can't stand off the might of an entire nation indefinitely. All of which means I must practice my written English, just like I must smile at all of the right people while attending all of the necessary parties.

For the first time in decades I find myself envying Jace and Katrina. They have none of the power or prestige that Kyle and I currently enjoy, but they have freedom. Kat has taken a human lover, a charming middle-aged cobbler whose head is positively spinning at the gifts and attention she lavishes upon him.

Jace...well, Jace is still Jace. He hasn't taken a mistress, hasn't been with any woman since he broke things off with that cow from Germany a hundred and fifty years ago, but he's taking advantage of his freedom in other ways. He's begun construction of a countryside manor that will be most impressive when it is done.

I suspect he mostly pursues it because it puts distance between us, but I also think he legitimately enjoys the work, enjoys mastering an architectural challenge in ways that the world has never seen before. Jace will never be a real researcher, but he does have a good mind and an even better heart.

I wish that he would find someone. If I had a shilling for every time I'd wished that he and Kat could be happy together I'd be...well, an even wealthier woman than I already am. I can't think of anything better than my two best friends experiencing the same happiness that I've been enjoying.

In other news, Kyle and I demonstrated the system-speeding effect that we've been working on to Jace and Kat. We only showed them how to reach a speed twice that of a normal person, but even that small crumb represents something that could be a huge advantage in the fight with Nikoli that Kyle is so concerned is coming.

Kat played down her excitement as she's done so often lately. Once she had mastered the effect she simply shrugged and named it time bending. It's a misnomer given that we aren't actually impacting the flow of time, but I didn't correct her. I'm just glad to see her excited about something.

Something happened in the retreat from Paris that she hasn't been willing to discuss with me.

I've tried to get her to open up, but so far I've been less than successful. I must take refuge in the fact that eventually it will be wiped clean, never again to be remembered. The forgetting is so often the bane of our existence—it's just too bad that it requires something so terrible to turn our curse into a positive.

If I were a different woman I would be tempted to find the journal where she's written the experience down and make arrangements for an accident to befall the relevant pages. It's the only way for her to ever forget what happened, but I know that would be a betrayal like none other. I will have to settle for the memory losing its strength at some point in the next hundred years or so.

I often think that there are too many secrets in this world. We hide our nature from the humans around us, and that is bad enough, but it is nothing in comparison to the secrets we keep from each other. In this regard I'm as guilty as the rest, for I've agreed with Kyle to hide the bulk of our research from the other two.

We provide them with the crumbs from our table while keeping the best of the feast for ourselves. Kyle's reasoning is sound, but I dislike the thought of Jace and Kat going into battle armed with less than the best we are capable of providing them. I worry that something will happen to one of them and our little family will be broken up for a season—possibly even forever. The world is a much smaller place than it once was, but there is still so much of it, a wide, terrifying place in which to find one single person.

I think I hear Kyle arriving downstairs. The footmen are all aflutter, which usually means that he's sent word on ahead. Yes, I can see his carriage coming up the street. I should go—he'll doubtlessly be worked up over something that happened at court, or barring that he'll want to discuss contingency plans in case Ashwell's group or Nikoli's group tries to eliminate us.

Before I go though there is just one more thing I should record. I had a conversation with Kat this morning, that I would hate to ever forget, but which I know will leave me all too soon.

I asked her if she loved her cobbler, if she would eventually tell him what she is. She told me she did, but that telling him would depend on whether she felt he could survive learning that the world was much broader than he'd always thought. I was prepared to leave things there, but she asked me if I doubted her love for Patrick, her cobbler.

It had never occurred to me to doubt her feelings, but I've known Kat for more than two hundred years. This wasn't about her and Patrick, this was about Kyle and me.

I've known for a long time that she doubts my decision, that she thinks that I picked the wrong brother, but this is the first time in decades that she's said as much. We argued and she stormed out as she so often does.

Thankfully I know she'll be back tomorrow and all will be forgiven, but I wish that I could make her see what I see in my Kyle. I had...not a realization exactly, more like a reminder of something that I've known for the longest time, but which I sometimes take for granted.

I could never be as happy with Jace as I am with Kyle. Jace is good and tender, considerate and kind. Any woman, highborn or low, would be lucky to have him, but he's not for me. Kyle is brilliant and powerful, but more than that, he's full of life and emotion. With Kyle I never have to worry that

I'm too much, that I feel too much, that my rage will lash out and hurt him.

Kyle is his own person, complete with or without me, powerful and shielded by a rage as strong as anything contained inside of me. Kyle is strong enough to allow me to be as strong as I could ever want to be. With Kyle I'll never have to stifle my potential, and I'll always have a mind that is my equal with which to share the burden of protecting our pantheon.

Kyle understands me in ways that Jace never will because in many ways he is me. We are two sides of the same coin and he sparks a desire inside of me so intense that it can't be described. I've been happy with Kyle for more decades than most people get in two or even three lifetimes.

Our fights are spectacular, but we always come back together in the end and I'm always glad that we do.

Chapter 15

I'd paged through a number of entries in French before making it to that first English entry, and when I surfaced from reading I felt like I'd run a marathon. There was something to her narrative that went beyond the words on the page.

The woman who had written that entry hadn't been able to imagine jet fighters, cell phones or the internet, but she'd likewise done and seen things that I couldn't wrap my mind around. Despite our differences, there were similarities between us that I hadn't expected to find. She was desperately loyal to her family, to the little pantheon that she'd spent so many years with, and she was terribly afraid of the burden that she was forced to carry.

She hadn't wanted to be a researcher any more than I did. She played with the forces of creation, risking her existence in the process, for one reason and one reason only. Because it was her best chance of keeping the people around her safe. And even then she wasn't sure that she was going to be smart enough or powerful enough to protect them.

She was just as worried that she was going to come up short as I was. She was worried about not being *enough*.

The lure of someone else to share that burden with was nearly overpowering to me three centuries later—there was no way she could have withstood that kind of temptation back then. I wasn't her though. I was tempted, but I also knew things she hadn't. I knew that I'd eventually picked Jace, and I knew that Kyle had turned into someone darker than he'd been, someone who researched solely for the power it brought him, someone willing to sacrifice Jace and Kat without a second thought—someone willing to sacrifice even me if it came to that.

I was shaking, as much from hunger and exhaustion as from the extreme emotions coursing through me, but I reached for the book again anyway. The next several entries were in French, which was depressing. If all of my journals were a mix of two or more languages, I was going to have to expand my knowledge of other languages a lot more than I'd ever planned on.

Sometimes it seemed like it was all I could do to read and write in my native tongue—the idea of trying to cram French into my head made me want to slit my wrists. Being some kind of all-powerful demigod was supposed to be fun; so far it had just been a lot of danger, and even more studying.

Kyle moved next to me under the comforter, and for a second I thought he was waking up, which would be good—except for the fact that the only thing I was wearing was one of his t-shirts. Now I had yet another reason to get out of bed, but I didn't. Instead I picked my journal back up and resumed flipping through the pages in search of something written in the only language I understood.

I was halfway through the book—and still hadn't found a second entry in English—when I realized that I was starting to get hot. I absently shoved the comforter away, and in the process my left hand brushed across the bare skin of Kyle's chest and I realized that he was burning up again.

It had to be the poison—nothing natural would have caused him to develop a fever again after the first one had finally broke—and I finally had to face the fact that I was the biggest idiot in the world. I'd wasted the last hour with a journal—most of which I couldn't even read—instead of doing the smart thing and getting some food into me.

I pushed my journal to the side and rolled out of bed and onto what had to be the world's shakiest feet. Under normal circumstances I wouldn't have had a prayer of getting Kyle to the bathtub, but I just reached for my anger—there was still plenty of it there for the asking—and amped up my strength to the point where it was a simple matter to grab Kyle's ankles and pull him toward me.

The bathroom was an absolute mess. I hadn't bothered to clean it up, my wet clothes were still piled on the floor and Kyle's jeans were still floating in the half-full tub. I fished his jeans out of the water and slung them over the nearby glass-walled shower in the three seconds it took me to climb into the water and submerge both of us.

The water was only a shade below room temperature, but Kyle started shivering instantly as the lukewarm water started sucking heat out of him. I turned the cold water on full and then pulled Kyle back on top of me, trying to conserve my energy.

Unfortunately once I was lying there motionless in the water there wasn't anything to distract me from the fact that I had one of the hottest guys in the world pressed up against me.

I started reciting a litany of Kyle's faults. He was selfish, he was cruel, and he was heartless. When that short list of character defects didn't serve to distract me from the feel of his rock-hard abs shaking underneath my right hand, I moved my hand higher up on his body and added to the list.

He was probably a bad kisser...only I didn't believe that. In fact, I didn't believe most of the things I was adding to the list, and as I acknowledged that truth I was forced to admit my doubts about the first three flaws on my list.

Pretending Kyle was someone other than who he was wasn't going to magically change his character for the worse any more than it would change his character for the better...any more than it would make the smooth, bulging pectorals underneath my hand anything other than swoon-worthy.

The truth was that Kyle's chest was as incredible as the narrow hips peeking out over the top of his boxers, and I had no idea what he was really like.

I moved my hand back down to his stomach and pulled him even closer to me. I told myself that I just wanted to be able to tell the instant his fever broke so that I could get him out of the water before his temperature plunged too far, but that was just an excuse.

"You'd better come back to me, Kyle. We've been through too much together for you to slip away before I've even had a chance to figure out which half of the story you're telling is the lie. You owe me that much. *I* owe you that much."

Chapter 16

By the time Kyle's fever broke again I was shaking even worse than he was. The water never got that cold—even with the tap going full out the entire time we were in the tub—but the temperature wasn't the only reason I was trembling.

Somewhere along the way I'd managed to tear myself away from the ache inside of me enough to realize just how dangerous of a situation I was in. I was developing feelings for Kyle that put everything I had with Jace in jeopardy, but none of that mattered if Fenrir and his henchmen broke through our wards sometime next week and killed Kyle and me.

As bad as that was, the threat of our wards collapsing didn't matter in the slightest if I let myself become too weak to take care of Kyle. If that happened then Fenrir would break in to find a couple of several-day-old corpses waiting for him.

I didn't know how I was going to accomplish everything that needed to be accomplished, but I had to at least try.

I got Kyle out of the water and dried him with one of the two remaining dry towels, the towels that I'd used as a blanket for him while I'd gone upstairs to get the comforter. Then I tucked him inside the comforter while I dried myself and pulled on another of his t-shirts.

There was no telling how many more cycles of freezing and fever we were in for, but if we didn't have dry towels then there wouldn't be any coming back the next time his fever broke. I grabbed all of the wet towels and my clothes and hung them over any surface I could find that looked like it might serve to dry them over the next few hours.

That took less than four minutes, but by the time I climbed into the bed with Kyle I was worried that I'd taken too long to get him warmed back up.

I had vague thoughts of trying to find the thermostat for this room, but it was all I could do to keep my eyes open while I cuddled next to Kyle's shivering body. Luckily, sheer exhaustion seemed to have at least temporarily cured me of the desire to lose myself in the thrill of running my hands up and down Kyle's muscly chest.

Based on the clock near Kyle's bed it took nearly an hour for him to warm back up to where he wasn't shivering, at which point I climbed out of bed and ran upstairs. I knew there were a couple of cans of soup left, but Kyle was going to need them.

I was more than a little worried that I was going to have to run back downstairs and harvest from the garden if I wanted to eat, but I didn't have that kind of time, so I was hoping that Kyle had stocked up on something else during one of his recent trips to the outside world.

I'd already checked the freezer so I knew there weren't any microwave meals hiding in there. I went through the rest of the cabinets that I hadn't checked the first time around when I'd been looking for the soup, and was nearly in a panic by the time I was halfway through still with no sign of any high-calorie processed food.

I did however find a couple of heating pads. They were the kind that you could put in the microwave, which gave me a great idea. I put the first blue square into the microwave and turned it on while I searched the rest of the cabinets for something I could eat.

Jackpot. About the same time the first heating pad came out of the microwave I found two boxes of cookies and tore into one of the sleeves of cookies like I was a starving savage—which was actually not too far from the truth.

I crammed three cookies into my mouth and then put the second heating pad into the microwave. My dad would have frowned and told me that cookies weren't a meal. Ari would have gasped and told me that they were going to go straight to my hips, but for the first time in my life I didn't have to worry about what I was eating. By that point I could have gone through both boxes in less than twenty-four hours and still not replaced the calories I'd lost shivering in the cold water with Kyle.

Speaking of which, I'd already been gone for too long. I zipped back downstairs with both heating pads, and after checking Kyle's temperature to make sure he hadn't spiked another fever, slipped the heating pads under the covers with him to help make up for the fact that I wasn't there with him.

I still wasn't free—not really. I still had to worry about Fenrir, and I still couldn't leave Kyle's side for very long without risking another sudden fever, but I was a lot more free than I'd been in hours.

I ran back upstairs for what I told myself was going to be the last time for a while and heated up one of the last two cans of soup. A few minutes later I was back downstairs with warm soup and cookies.

Feeding Kyle hadn't exactly gotten any easier, but at least now I knew what to expect. He got all of the chicken broth and I finished up the noodles to balance out my meal of cookies. I tried really hard at first to keep from getting crumbs everywhere, but then the ludicrousness of it all caught up with me and I decided if Kyle complained about some cookie crumbs when he woke up—if he woke up—then I would just strangle him myself.

Once we were both fed I wanted nothing more than to just fall asleep and never wake up, but I forced myself to take the opportunity to prep for future emergencies. I broke my promise to myself and went back upstairs again, but this time I swapped out my dirty dishes for clean dishes, the last can of soup, the can opener, and the microwave.

I probably made quite the sight lugging it all downstairs inside of the microwave, but it all fit perfectly once I cleared off one of the end tables and it meant that I could warm up a heating pad without ever even having to leave the bed. In my mind that was worth looking stupid, especially when there wasn't anyone around to see it.

I debated cleaning myself up, but in the end exhaustion won out. I fished the heating pads out and crawled under the comforter with Kyle. I was still too tired to turn into an over-sexed lust bunny, but that didn't mean that it didn't feel nice to wrap my arms around his bare chest and stomach.

Too bad I fell asleep before I really had a chance to appreciate my situation.

Chapter 17

I'd fallen asleep prepared for a sudden change in Kyle's core temperature to force me out of bed after just a few hours. Instead, I actually managed to get a full six hours of sleep. If I'd been human that wouldn't have been anywhere near enough, but as an Awakened I'd basically just slept for twenty-four hours straight.

My journal was waiting for me on the edge of the bed when I woke up. It was tempting—even more tempting than the half-naked man sleeping next to me—but I wasn't sure I could handle any more revelations. I was already struggling when it came to my self-control. It wasn't like I was really going to assault Kyle while he was sleeping, but the things that I was feeling right now were going to make things difficult once he woke up.

Another journal entry or two talking about how Kyle was the perfect boyfriend—the perfect husband—wasn't going to make things any easier.

In the end I heated up both of the heating pads and then rolled out of bed and headed into the bathroom for a long overdue shower. It was the most awkward morning ritual I'd ever performed. I kept coming out of the bathroom half-dressed or midway through brushing my teeth to check on Kyle, and it took a lot longer than I'd expected it to, but when I was finally done I looked at least somewhat presentable and I felt a ton better.

My clothes were dry, but they weren't exactly clean, so I pulled on another of Kyle's t-shirts and then hunted around downstairs until I managed to find the decades-old washing machine and dryer. It was silly to run it with just my clothes, so I grabbed some of Kyle's laundry from the pile the chute deposited them in, and threw them in too.

By that point I'd been out of bed and left Kyle unattended for the longest single stretch since he'd been injured. I was super nervous I was going to come back and find him burning up again, but if anything when I made it back to the bedroom he was starting to get a little cold.

I reheated the heating packs and propped them up against his chest and back, and looked over at the innocent-looking white leather of Genevieve's journal. Talk about tempting. I told myself I was better than that, popped a couple of cookies in my mouth, and left the room.

I headed downstairs planning on getting some fruits and vegetables, but I ended up stopping off in Kyle's lab. It was hard to say what pulled me there. I would have expected it to be the egg-shaped pseudo-artifact, but once I made it inside I just ended up staring at all of the equations on his chalk boards.

It was funny. My mind usually shut down when faced with anything more complicated than $3x = 9$. I wasn't that girl, that woman, who'd spent decades unlocking the secrets of the universe. I knew less than nothing about what any of Kyle's equations meant, but they still somehow looked right to me.

Rather, most of them looked right to me. I felt like the amnesia patient who'd been told that she was still capable of doing routine, familiar mechanical tasks if she didn't think about it. It was like I'd been handed a pen and I'd signed my name, but while the signature looked right I didn't know what I'd just signed or who I actually was.

I walked past blackboard after blackboard that looked utterly alien and yet still completely familiar, but the last two looked wrong somehow. I must have stood there for almost twenty minutes before remembering that I was on a deadline. After that I hurried the rest of the way down to the garden and picked an assortment of fruits.

I stopped off at Kyle's bedroom on the way back upstairs to check on him and reheat the heating pads, but he seemed to be doing all right so I went on up to the kitchen and washed the fruit clean. The ancient, industrial-sized blender that I'd seen on one of my earlier trips was more than up to pulping the fruits and I managed to find honest-to-goodness refined sugar and added half a cup into the mix to give it some extra calories.

I probably would have added in ice except for the fact that the ice cube trays were still down in Kyle's bathroom. I would have felt like a terrible house guest if not for the fact that I was dealing with such extenuating circumstances. It was hard to feel guilty about trashing Kyle's place when I'd been playing round-the-clock nurse for the last two days.

The last forty-eight hours had been some of the most exhausting of my life. I was worn out, half-starved, and wound more tightly than I'd ever been wound, but it had also been incredibly satisfying—especially the last few hours. It just felt right to be taking care of Kyle.

It was kind of funny. Here we were three hundred years after Genevieve's journal entry had been written. Women could vote now and own property, but this version of me had probably done more 'women's work' in the last two days than the last version had done in a decade. She'd been nobility. It didn't matter whether she'd been born that way or if she'd used transmuted gold to buy her way in, the pantheon had probably never lacked for anything. She'd had servants who'd taken care of the cooking and the cleaning.

I was none of those things. Maybe eventually I'd end up being today's equivalent, but for now I was enjoying playing house. Maybe that was the key all along. This was my choice, and as long as it continued to be a choice rather than something forced upon me, I'd still continue to take some measure of enjoyment in it.

I ran the blender one more time, liquefying the fruit mixture, and then I poured it all into two tall glasses and grabbed a spoon before heading back downstairs. It was tarter than I expected, but it was still good. I spooned it into Kyle's mouth a little bit at a time, finished mine off and then settled in next to him.

I didn't even try to resist the pull of my journal. Maybe I was being stupid. I was definitely risking what I had with Jace, but I just had to know what it had been like. Most people had to jump into a relationship and just hope that things would work out. I, on the other hand, could get a sneak peek at how everything had turned out the last time around.

It just didn't seem right to pass that chance up. I couldn't have both Jace and Kyle—I wasn't even sure that I wanted both—and in a lot of ways reading my old journal was going to make things harder. Making a decision knowing exactly what I was giving up by picking one of them and rejecting the other, was going to be difficult, but not looking felt wrong. I'd always thought that in my own way I was as brave as anyone else—I'd had to be to survive after my mom died. I wasn't going to take the coward's way out now.

Journal Entry
May 29, 1729

I often come back to my journals and reread them, but never with as much fervency as when I'm faced with a difficult choice. I failed Kyle. I've tried for nearly five years to tell myself otherwise, but the truth is that I did.

He was right about so much, so many things that I didn't want to accept. Maybe that is why I lapsed back into French for so long. There was no good reason. French is no more tolerated here in the colonies than it was back in London. There was no reason to return to my native tongue other than the fact that it was my mind's way of trying to assert my correctness, of trying to stick to my way despite all of the evidence that my way was wrong.

Kyle was right to be worried about Ashwell, and I was right to be worried about Nikoli's transplants. Jace has told me a hundred times that it wasn't my fault, that I couldn't have foreseen the two closest pantheons uniting against us, but he's wrong. I should have foreseen the possibility, and spent more time in court in an effort to head it off.

IMMORTAL

These aren't the same times we were born into. We aren't worshiped as gods anymore. That gives us more freedom, but it also means that we are at the mercy of the humans. Really that was always the case, we just refused to admit it back then.

I'm unaware of any instance where a pantheon from the old days was assassinated without first having their human empires overthrown. I was so smug about the new way of things, about our superiority over the humans, that I ignored Kyle's worries.

I should have been out there molding society to my whim, creating allies and informants rather than wasting my time in research that I knew we wouldn't unveil for decades to come. I indulged myself in a pointless hobby instead of doing my duty to our little family, and as a result we lost everything.

Jace lost his mansion, the marvel of muscle and design that was the talk of the entire court. Kat lost her cobbler—Patrick—struck down in a needless attempt to defend her from powers he couldn't understand. Kyle lost his memories, all of the knowledge and wisdom gathered over the course of centuries wiped away over the course of one hour of fighting, one hour that killed tens of thousands of innocents and three of our true enemies, one hour that will no doubt go down in the history books as a great fire or a limited outbreak of the plague.

I foolishly thought that, out of all of us, I was the only one not to have lost anything. I thought *that we would just travel to the new world and pick back up where we'd left off, that Kyle would come back to me over the weeks and months that followed.*

I was such a fool. Something changed. Maybe it was the result of sustaining an emotional peak capable of burning through so many memories in such a short time. Kyle couldn't have sustained such a drawdown of power out of anger. I always assumed that he tapped into one of the stronger positive emotions, but I've come to wonder since then. Maybe he tapped into something darker and it left behind an unwanted mark on his very soul.

Maybe not. Maybe it's as simple as starting what amounted to a new life in a world infinitely more dangerous than the one we once knew. The fall of the great empires was good for the humans. It meant that fewer of them have to die at our command or because of our actions, but it means that conflicts among our kind happen with breathtaking speed.

There isn't any more gradual tilt as one economy weakens and begins to crack under the strain of supporting a war. There's no series of reverses as one side slowly pushes the other side out of massive fortifications.

There's nothing left to barter with. With the discovery of transmutation, gold is worthless other than as a motivator to get the humans to serve us. The only thing the other pantheons want now is our knowledge and our lives.

IMMORTAL

Whatever the reason, the Kyle sleeping three doors down from me is nothing at all like the Kyle who guided us out of Paris and tried to secure a position in the English court. He's darker, and if anything he believes my sins are virtues.

He wants to leave the rest of the world behind, to spend all of our time researching, to create a weapon capable of enslaving all other pantheons, of forcing every human into servitude and creating an empire that will span the entire globe.

I've tried to show him a different way, tried to explain that there are other things in life more important than the pursuit of knowledge, but he doesn't trust me anymore. He doesn't even trust his own journals.

I thought I was making progress, but tonight he gave me an ultimatum. I have to pick between him and the others. He thinks that my refusal is because I have feelings for his brother.

I do, but not in the way that he thinks. Kat and Jace have been loyal to our pantheon for centuries. Kat was with me even before I found Kyle and Jace. How can I leave my family for a stranger whose rage has become so powerful that he's even willing to resort to violence to silence me?

I can't, even though I know Kyle will walk out of our lives tomorrow morning and I may never see him again. It's only fitting that I write this in his native language rather than mine.

In time I will forget every moment I've spent with the love of my life. In time he will be nothing *more than a name and some dry facts. I fully expect at some point we will become enemies. I pray it will not be so, but in my heart I know this version of Kyle is even more dangerous than the one I knew and loved. He has all of the old Kyle's intellect and none of his humanity.*

Unless another pantheon succeeds in stopping him first, Kyle will eventually become a threat to the entire human race. When that day comes I will be unable to just stand to one side and watch as he slaughters all who oppose him. Maybe once I could have, but Kat and Jace have shown me a different way. They've shown me the value of even the least of our cousins and I cannot help but fight for them, even at the cost of my life if necessary.

And so I'm leaving this message to whatever future version of myself might read it. Kyle is the way he is because of my mistake—our mistake. Do whatever you can to bring him back from the edge if you get the chance. If you don't, you're going to end up having to kill him to save people you care about.

Chapter 18

I closed the book with more force than I'd intended on using and then regretted doing so. I'd been right to be scared of what this journal had contained, but I didn't want to destroy it. Three hundred year-old books weren't exactly indestructible.

Still, I wasn't going to go back and read more of the entries—assuming any of them were even in English—anytime soon. I didn't need the last version of me messing with my head any more than she already had. I needed to get back to Jace and Kat, and I needed to read one of my more recent journals, something from the time when Jace and I had been happily in love. Only now I was wondering if we'd really been as happy as I'd initially thought.

Jace had as much as warned me that he'd always been the one who pursued me. What if I'd just settled for him after I'd realized that I was never going to be able to make things work out with the new, darker Kyle?

It was all too much for my seventeen-year-old brain. I should be worrying about who was going to take me to prom and how I was going to be able to afford the dress I wanted, not contemplating choosing between two guys I had hundreds of years of history with.

I took a deep breath, maybe to scream, maybe just because I thought it would calm me down, and then I realized that Kyle's breathing had changed. Even before I turned my head to look I knew he was awake, but I turned to make sure. Perfect, soft gray eyes looked back up at me. I felt my skin go hot from embarrassment and started to move my hand away from his bare skin, but he trapped it against his stomach with his hand.

"How long have I been out?"

"I'm not positive. I think it's been two days. How much do you remember?"

I tried to keep my voice calm, but my heart was trying to pound its way out of my chest. It was hard to know how much of that was from the thrill of touching him, and how much of it was concern over whether his fever had caused some kind of brain damage.

"I'm not sure, it's still coming back to me. We...we were fighting outside of the...third ward?"

I nodded and he continued. "We were doing pretty well until a pooka and some kind of flying monkey snake showed up. You used a peak memory to burn a big piece out of Fenrir and then both of us burned additional peak memories to kill Fenrir, but not before he got his teeth on me."

I wasn't sure how to interpret Kyle's response so far. It had seemed pretty promising until he'd called the smallest Unseelie fae a flying monkey snake. Maybe he really had lost chunks of his memory due to running such a high temperature.

Luckily Kyle hadn't noticed my concern. "I remember healing myself and realizing that I'd been poisoned. What are my symptoms?"

"Your core temperature has been all over the place. One minute you're freezing to death and then in the next you're running a raging fever."

Kyle looked confused for a second and then nodded in understanding. "You had a hard time keeping me from overheating and you were worried that there was permanent brain damage."

"Well, you did call the one fae a pooka and the other a flying monkey snake. That's not exactly in keeping with the way you usually talk..."

Kyle shrugged. "Not all of the Unseelie fae have been categorized the way that you'd think."

"So you're really all here?"

"Yeah, I think so. Did you miss me?"

There was something to his question that I hadn't expected. Two days ago I would have dismissed the question as nothing more than a joke, but now I could see that there was more to it than that. There had always been more to it than that.

I wanted to say yes, wanted to tell him that I'd missed him desperately and not just because he was my only way out. The desire was so strong that I almost gave in, but at the last second Jace's face swam across my field of vision. If I gave in to my feelings for Kyle there wouldn't be any going back.

I owed it to Jace to find out how things had really been between us, to tell him what was going on inside of my head. I knew Kyle would sense it if I lied though, so I did the next best thing. I pulled my hand away from his bare skin and smiled.

"Of course I missed you. This place is one big tomb just waiting for one or both of us to drop over dead. I would have killed to have anyone to talk to."

That threw him off. I could see him questioning his Spidey sense, see him trying to separate fact from fiction, but I met his eyes without flinching.

"It looks like you found your journal..."

"Yeah, you mentioned it at one point in between hallucinations."

"What do you think?"

He was just too damn shrewd. I should have known better than to try to bluff someone who remembered the better part of the last two hundred years. It was time to change the topic.

"I think we need to figure out where we go from here. Fenrir is probably just about ready to take down the next ward. We're running out of time before he'll be battering down our doors and I don't fancy fighting him inside here. How long before you can heal yourself and get back out there?"

There was a flicker of something in the back of his eyes at the way I'd started my response. He'd thought I meant that we needed to figure out where *we* were going to go. The couple version of we.

I felt like such a fool. It had been there all along if I'd only known what to look for. He'd been in love with me since even before I'd arrived back here. That was all well and good in fairytales, but that would never work in real life. I was never going to be as good as whatever it was he had built up in his mind.

I'd known that I was starting to fall for Kyle, but I hadn't realized how hard until that exact moment. A tremor started deep inside me and I realized how crushed I was that there wasn't even a *chance* of us being together.

It was stupid. I had Jace—I didn't need anything or anyone else. Jace was perfect in every way and I shouldn't need the chance of things working out with Kyle to get me through the day.

I forced a smile onto my face and prayed that it was good enough to fool the guy who'd spent the last two hundred years poring over journals containing every interaction we'd ever had with each other.

"I think we still have a chance. I understand how to use my peak memories now, and I've got seventeen years of them stored up. This time I won't screw around, if I cut loose with that kind of attack right off the bat I should be able to take down the horse and the flying monkey snake while you keep Fenrir distracted."

There was genuine regret in Kyle's eyes as he shook his head. Had he realized it wasn't going to work out between us?

"It won't work, Selene"

"No, it has to work! My friends and family are depending on me getting out of here and meeting back up with them. My dad will *die* if we can't find a way to beat Fenrir. If this is about you having to use more peak memories, I'll owe you. Whatever you want. You want my help researching so that you can develop a real artifact? It's yours. You want me chained here for the next forty years as your personal maid and cook? Done. Just please help me."

Kyle reached up and grabbed my hands. He shouldn't have been strong enough to do that. I hadn't felt him amp himself, but it was the only explanation for my complete inability to move my arms.

"It's not that, Selene. I would gladly help you, but the venom is still in my system. I don't know how to heal it—not really. Maybe my brother would be able to figure it out in the time we have left, but the human body isn't my area of expertise. Without knowing exactly how it's messing with my metabolism, anything I do could just make things worse."

What little strength I had left me as I acknowledged defeat. I was no match for Fenrir by myself, especially not now that he had help. I opened my mouth to tell Kyle it was over, and then I realized that I'd spent days looking at the problem the wrong way.

"If you can't fight then we'll just have to get some help. Kat and I gave Fenrir a run for his money before. With Jace to help out we shouldn't have any problem kicking Fenrir's teeth in until he's as small as the snake monkey."

"Absolutely not."

"Excuse me?"

Kyle looked at me with eyes so full of rage I almost couldn't breathe. "I will not be saved by my brother. I swore that I would never help him, that I would never accept help from him. He betrayed me once, I will never again put myself in a position where he can hurt me like that."

"You are not going to let my father die because of what happened between the three of us two hundred years ago."

"You chose him over me, Selene. I sacrificed everything I was to protect the three of you. I needed you, but you just used me up and cast me aside like I was nothing more than a piece of garbage!"

"No. I refuse to believe that. I read the journal entry. I wanted to make things right between the two of us, *you* were the one who made me choose between them and you."

"I was your *husband*. I had every right to make you choose."

Up until that moment I'd been fighting to remain calm, fighting not to lose my temper. That stopped as soon as he played the marriage card. I climbed out of bed and opened myself up to the rage.

"No, my husband died fighting off two enemy pantheons that day. I honored his sacrifice and I tried to make things right between us, but you weren't him, you weren't even a shadow of him."

"You read the French entries."

"No. I didn't have to."

Even as I said it I wasn't sure what I meant by it, but Kyle recoiled as though he'd been slapped. I turned and headed towards the stairwell.

"Where are you going?"

"I'm going to phone a friend."

"I won't give you the password to the computer."

I turned back to him and gave him a smile that would have frozen a bonfire. "You don't have to, I already know it."

Chapter 19

Kyle tried to get out of bed and follow me, but he was too weak. He collapsed onto the carpet, and I didn't stop walking when he called out to me.

A few seconds later I was sitting down at Kyle's computer. I put four numbers into the password box that popped up. Zero, three, one and four. March fourteenth.

I didn't realize I'd been holding my breath until it worked and the home screen popped up. Kyle had been using my birthday as his password because it was the one thing he never forgot.

I found an internet calling program and dialed Jace's phone number. The thought of talking to Jace made my heart flutter with something that was part guilt and part anticipation. I told myself that there wasn't any reason to get freaked out. The call wouldn't be coming from a number that he recognized, so there was every reason to believe that Jace wouldn't even pick up. It was the only thing keeping me in my chair.

"Hello?"

His voice sounded different, deeper and drawn out, but that was just the result of the two of us operating at different speeds. He was experiencing time only half as fast as I was. He sounded different, but it was still Jace.

My knees went weak and tears started pooling in the corners of my eyes. It was a good thing I was already sitting down. The sound of his voice was like coming home after being away for years. If I'd had any doubt about whether or not I loved him, that would have settled it.

"Jace? It's me—Selene."

"Selene! I'm so relieved that you're still alive. Where are you? We've been trying to find you everywhere…"

"I know. I would have called sooner, but it just wasn't possible. How are you? Are Kat and Ari okay?"

"Yeah, the three of us are fine, but your dad—"

"I know, Mephistoles has him."

Jace didn't ask how I knew, he just kept on, moving to the next thing that he knew I'd want to know. It wasn't that he didn't have questions of his own, he just cared about my happiness more than he did about getting his answers.

"We've been trying to come up with a way to go get him, but Mephistoles isn't just any run-of-the-mill bad guy. He's got a necklace that allows him to sustain higher, more extended emotional peaks. His only limiting factor is how much in the way of memories he has to burn in any given fight. It makes him stronger than any one or even two of us."

"Of course, he has an artifact."

"How did you know that?"

For the first time I realized how sticky this conversation was going to get. "Kyle told me. I don't know how much Kat remembers, but it wasn't me who disembodied Fenrir. Kyle showed up at the last instant and saved us. He cut Fenrir's head off and then carried me back to his…home."

"If he's been keeping you captive I'll come tear his arms off and bury him under a mountainside."

I wasn't sure that I'd ever heard Jace mad before. Not like this, not so angry that he probably couldn't have summoned his default emotion even if his life had depended on it.

"It's not like that, Jace. I mean maybe it was at first, but I've been free to leave if I wanted to for a while now. The problem is that Fenrir followed us back here and he's pissed that Kyle interfered. Mephistoles was here for a while too, which is how I know he has my dad, but he left after they brought down the first two wards.

"By that point Kyle had rekeyed all of the other wards. I could have made a run for it, but I knew that wouldn't guarantee anything so I decided to stay here and fight. I figured Mephistoles wouldn't do anything to my dad as long as he knew that Fenrir had me boxed up, and it was better to weaken Fenrir before I came to help you get my dad back."

"This was never about you, Selene. I'm sorry. You're important to us, but all Mephistoles wants is your journals. We're down to less than twenty-four hours before we're supposed to deliver them to him and whoever he has helping him."

It felt like someone had put their fist into my chest and grabbed hold of my heart. "Even if you give him the journals he isn't going to let my dad go, is he?"

"We have to at least try."

"No, I understand at least a little how important those journals are. I need you and Kat to come here. Together the three of us can take down Fenrir and his two buddies. Then we can go after Mephistoles."

"Fenrir has help?"

The doubt in Jace's voice told me I was fighting a losing battle, but I gamely pressed on.

"Yeah, some kind of flying monkey thing and a horse with claws and fangs. It's okay though, I know how to create a sun lance now and I've figured out how to burn peak memories too. Kyle and I killed Fenrir by ourselves."

"It's not going to work, Selene. I wish it could, but it won't. Even if you're right and the three of us manage to put Fenrir down, we won't have enough juice to take down Mephistoles. Even at our best, the most Kat and I could hope to do is fight him to a standstill. That still leaves you to deal with whoever is helping him all by yourself."

"We have to do something, Jace. If the three of us can't make it happen then we need to find some help. What about the police?"

"They're no good. They'd have all kinds of questions that we couldn't answer. Not only that, once they saw the five of us fighting they'd be just as likely to start shooting at us as at Mephistoles. What...what about Kyle?"

"No, I already thought of that. The last time we fought Fenrir he managed to get his fangs on Kyle. Kyle healed the damage, but he couldn't do anything about the poison from the bite. He's awake now, but he's not going to be up to fighting any time soon."

"I've never heard any reports about Fenrir having venom."

"Yeah, Kyle was surprised too. Is that important?"

"It means that Fenrir has been concealing the true extent of his power for decades."

"He's been disembodied twice in the last two days, and the second time was *after* he bit Kyle. Maybe he's lost that particular ability."

I knew I sounded desperate, but I couldn't help myself. It was only fair for Jace to know the full extent of what he would be getting into if he came to help me, but I was terrified that he was going to back out.

"I'm not going to just leave you there, Selene, and we aren't going to let Mephistoles kill your dad without a fight. Give me an hour or so to make some calls and then call me back. There might be a way we can use this to our advantage."

Chapter 20

I hung up with an acidic mixture of hope and fear still swirling around in my stomach. An hour for Jace would be two hours for me. Two hours was too long to avoid facing the music. I was going to have to go back downstairs and talk to Kyle.

I took a deep breath and headed to the stairwell. I opened the door expecting Kyle to yell at me from the bed, or maybe even from where I'd left him on the floor, but he wasn't in either place. Concern shot through me as I ran into the bathroom. He was there, unconscious, one arm dangling in the water, and he was burning up with fever.

I amped my strength up to three times normal without even thinking about it, and pulled Kyle into the water with me. Even through the thin layer of my shirt I could feel the heat radiating off of him, and the places where we were touching skin-to-skin were even worse. My arm especially felt like it was going to come away with actual burns.

The temptation to let go and save myself from the pain was intense, but I refused. Instead, I turned on the cold water and alternated which arm was holding him so that I at least spread the pain out.

I lost track of time. I forgot about calling Jace back, forgot about Fenrir and Mephistoles, even forgot about my dad. My whole world narrowed down to the slow, labored rise and fall of Kyle's chest and the distance between the top of the water and the top of the tub.

I held onto Kyle, I drained water out of the tub when it got too high, and I prayed. I prayed that Kyle would be okay, that he would come back from this and still be himself.

For the first time since he'd locked me away inside of his bunker, I didn't need him. Jace and Kat were going to come save me and then they were going to help me rescue my father. I didn't need Kyle to help me fight Fenrir, I didn't need him to help me fight Mephistoles, I didn't need anything from him at all, and that destroyed the last of my illusions.

Maybe at the beginning it had all been about what Kyle could do for me, but somewhere along the way that had all changed. I needed Kyle to survive because I cared about him and despite everything that had happened I still wanted to know if there was a chance for us to be together.

My arms were throbbing and red, and they ached like I'd been lifting weights for hours, but I refused to let go, refused to give up hope. I just closed my eyes and listened to the sound of his breathing.

I didn't remember falling asleep, but the next thing I knew I could feel him shift in my arms. I opened my eyes to find him facing me. I wanted to look away, but I forced myself to meet his gaze.

"I'm sorry I left you down here all by yourself. I shouldn't have done that while the poison was still in your system."

"No, you were right to go call my brother. I should have let you call him days ago. I want you here, but I want you here out of your own free will."

"Kyle, I can't——"

He stopped me with a finger to my lips. "Just let me finish and then you can say whatever it is you need to say. I told you some of the promises that I'd made myself, but I didn't tell you all of them. It's not all just about furthering the advancement of knowledge or hating my brother. Two hundred years ago, I hit you when you told me that you were going to choose Jace and Kat over me. It was the first and only time that had ever happened.

"I've checked my journals, but I didn't need to read them to know that——the sense of betrayal in your eyes would have told me as much. The very first promise I made myself, even before the other two, was that I would never strike you again, that I would never let the anger take over so fully again.

"I left the three of you behind and tried to make a new life for myself, but I never stopped thinking about you, Selene. When Mephistoles cornered you and Kat in New York I tried to tell myself that I'd done the only thing I could, but no matter how tightly I wove the logic of my argument it never felt right, so I made myself a new promise. I promised that I would never again let you be killed if there was something I could do to stop it.

"That is why you're here. All the rest of the things I told you, all of that business about wanting you to help me with my research, were just lies that I told myself to justify bringing you here. I don't deserve to say that I love you, but I do. Please stay with me."

My heart once again felt like it was going to batter its way right out of my chest, but this time it had nothing to do with his wet, glistening skin, or the way that his boxers rode low on his hips, or the inverted triangle formed by the muscles running from his waist to his shoulders.

This time it had everything to do with hundreds of years of feelings, feelings I didn't remember, feelings that had happened to someone else in a different body, in a different time, but which I'd somehow tapped into just by reading about them in a book.

It had nothing to do with his chiseled, perfect jaw and everything to do with the fact that I wanted him in ways that I'd never wanted anyone else other than Jace. Other than the brother he hated.

"Kyle, I—"

This time he stopped me not with his finger but with his lips. He reached down and pulled me up to him with one hand while the other gripped the side of the tub. He lifted me out of the water and pressed me against him as his lips molded themselves to mine.

He was surprisingly gentle, but there was an urgency to his movements. My shirt had come up far enough that his hand was pressed against the bare skin of my back and I was incredibly glad that this time I'd put on a pair of his old running shorts.

His hand on my skin felt like fire, but it was a good kind of fire, a burning that I never wanted to stop. I reached up and wrapped my arms around his neck, pulling him down with me into the water. We were both shaking, either from the cold or from simple exhaustion, but neither of us seemed willing to let that interrupt our kiss.

Kyle's body pressed against mine was the only thing keeping me warm, and he seemed to feel the same way about me. The tremble had reached my lips and I broke away from him gasping for air, but he just took the opportunity to switch targets and I felt his teeth close gently on my ear.

It sent me over the moon, under other circumstances it was the kind of thing that I never would have wanted to stop, but it was too much, too soon. I wasn't capable of resisting that kind of ecstasy for very long, and I'd just remembered that I wasn't entirely my own woman.

In that moment I desperately wanted Kyle, but I knew that I would eventually come down and regret how much this was going to hurt Jace.

"Stop, we have to stop."

Kyle pulled back, but his teeth were only fractions of a millimeter away from my skin and I knew he wanted to keep going, that he wanted to silence my protests with his mouth, but he was more of a gentleman than I'd realized. He pulled back, putting inches between us.

"You're sure?"

"It's not fair. It's not fair to you or him either one."

"Don't worry about my feelings or his feelings, Selene. What is it that you want?"

I let out a choppy sigh and refused to cry. I wasn't the victim here. However hard my decision was, it was nothing compared to what Kyle and Jace were going through.

"I don't know what I want anymore. Before you saved me from Fenrir I would have said that Jace was all I could ever want."

Kyle's knuckles went white on the tub next to my head, but I plowed on, desperate to finish.

"Now I've had a chance to read that journal and get a glimpse of what our life was like before we came to America. You scare me sometimes, and I don't agree with most of what you believe, but that glimpse is incredibly appealing. I feel your potential, Kyle. You have the ability to do great things and I want to be part of that. I can't make a decision without seeing what it was like when I was with Jace though. I need time to study, time to get to know you both better and think about what it is I really want."

Kyle looked away from me for several seconds and then nodded. "I understand. You have to do what you have to do, but you need to understand that things between the three of us are never going to be like they would be for normal people. There is too much history there. I'm never going to agree to pick you up on Friday knowing you're going out with him on Saturday."

Kyle was shivering so hard it was starting to affect his speech. His body was depleted in ways most people would never experience. His reserves were gone, he was exhausted and he was dangerously cold, but he refused to allow his weaknesses to define him. His will was more powerful than all that, and right now his will was entirely bent on convincing me that he was the one that I wanted.

"Come on, we need to get you dry and warmed back up or you'll go into shock again."

He looked for a second like he was going to argue, to say something else, but in the end he just nodded and started climbing out of the tub. He only made it halfway out before his arms gave out on him. I managed to grab one of his arms and stop him from hitting his head, but he still hit hard enough that he was going to have bruises.

"You idiot. If you're still that weak what were you doing kissing me?"

"I had to show you that I was more than just that guy, more than just research and world domination."

"I thought you thought those things were important."

Kyle didn't respond for several seconds while I toweled his back and chest dry.

"I did—I still do. I guess somewhere along the way I decided that you are even more important."

It was music to my ears. That was exactly what I wanted to hear, but I sternly told myself that it would have to wait, that I wasn't in a position to be making any decisions yet.

I amped my strength back up as I slung one of his arms over my shoulder and half carried, half dragged him to the bed. I once again threw a towel down to protect the comforter and then I dried his legs. He tried to help, but his movements were so weak it was nothing to just bat his hands away. I slipped one of the heating pads in the microwave and then slid Kyle into place and covered him with the comforter.

"I'll be back in a second to put the other one in."

"Thank you, Selene."

"It's just part of the routine by now—no need to thank me."

"No. I do need to thank you, and for more than just the heating pad. I would have died several times over if you hadn't been here to take care of me."

"It's only fair considering that you were hurt saving my life."

"Which I only had to do because you had just finished saving mine..."

That drew a smile out of me. "Okay, maybe we should just call it even."

Kyle nodded tiredly and settled back against the pillows as the microwave dinged. I pulled the heating pad out and slipped it under the covers before putting the second one in the microwave.

"We can call it even, but I still get to say thank you for showing me a different way, for bringing me back to something more like the man I was before."

"That I'll accept."

I gave him another smile and then headed downstairs to get my clothes. By the time I got back with my load of laundry, Kyle was already asleep. I slipped into the bathroom and pulled the door shut behind me.

IMMORTAL

I managed to get all the way dressed before the magnitude of my betrayal really hit. What was I thinking? Jace was never going to forgive me.

Chapter 21

When I came out of the bathroom twenty minutes later I'd washed away all the evidence of my tears, but I still wasn't sure how I was going to look Kyle in the eyes if he was awake once again. Luckily I didn't have to. He was asleep, shivering, but asleep.

He'd managed to get the second hot pack out of the microwave before he fell asleep, but apparently that hadn't been enough to keep him warm. I cycled both hot packs through the microwave, turning it off each time before it could chime to signal that it was done, and then tucked Kyle in with a source of heat on either side of him.

The trip up to the computer room was one of the hardest things I could remember doing. It felt like my legs each weighed a thousand pounds, but I knew that was just the weight of my guilt.

I unlocked the computer and checked the call log. It had been almost three hours in my time since I'd called Jace the first time, which meant that he'd had an hour and a half to make whatever arrangements he'd wanted to make. Not that he was still going to be willing to come help me once he knew I'd kissed Kyle.

I took a deep breath and dialed Jace's number again.

"Hello?"

"Kat, is that you? Where's Jace?"

"He's running Ari down to the vault in our basement. We only have the one ward because we didn't want to attract the wrong kind of attention, but it should still be enough to keep her safe from Mephistoles while we are gone."

"How long before he'll be back? I'd like to talk to him."

"I don't know. Where are you located?"

I pulled up a web browser and did a web search. "It says that my internet provider is in Southern Wyoming. Will that be enough?"

"I'm not sure. It will at least be enough to get us started moving though. Once we are closer we'll probably be able to feel the ward, but given how short our timetable is for getting back down here to save your dad, we could probably use some directions."

"Right, I'll work on getting you some better directions the next time Kyle wakes up."

There was silence on the line for several seconds.

"Well, if that's all, we'll just wait for you to call us back with directions."

"That—well, that isn't everything, but I guess I'll call back later when I can hopefully catch Jace."

"You kissed Kyle, didn't you, Selene?"

"How did you know?"

"I've been your friend for more than four centuries. I don't remember most of it, but I know what it means when you break out that voice. That's your serious guilt voice. You don't use that for anything small."

"Yeah, I kissed him. I don't know what I was thinking, it just kind of happened. I need to talk to Jace about it though. It doesn't seem fair for him to come risk his life without knowing what I did."

Kat sighed. "I should have seen this coming. All right, here's what we're going to do. You aren't going to tell Jace anything until after we've dealt with Fenrir. It would be even better if you could keep your big mouth shut until after we've rescued your dad, but I suspect that's going to be asking too much.

"We'll put Fenrir down, or more likely disembody him, then you and Jace can have your big blowup in the car on the way back here. It will be uncomfortable as hell, but it's a better option and I don't think that Jace is petty enough to let your dad die out of spite."

"No! Kat, I can't hide this from him. I need to tell him—as soon as possible. It's the right thing to do."

"No, Selene, this is about more than just you and Jace. That isn't the right thing to do, it's just the thing that's most likely to give you a shot at fixing the mess you've made. The right thing to do is kick some wolf butt and then save your dad. Once that is done, you and Jace can try to salvage whatever is left of your social life."

"You can't stop me, Kat. I'm going to call him back."

"Correction, you're going to call his phone back, a phone that is going to conveniently be off for the next hour or two. Trust me when I say that it's going to stay in my pocket for that entire time."

"I'll call your phone."

"No, you won't. If you do that you'll just be forcing me to turn *my* phone off, which will drastically reduce the odds of us actually finding you in time to save your dad."

"I guess you've thought of everything."

"Yeah, I guess after three hundred years of watching you make a mess out of your social life I've gotten pretty good at damage control. You can thank me later, once you've had a chance to see that I'm right. Don't bother calling me until you have directions."

Chapter 22

It was probably a good thing that I was calling using Kyle's computer rather than on a cell phone. It was a lot harder to throw a computer across the room. I could've amped my strength up to the point where it was still possible, but it wasn't worth the effort. Besides, I was going to need all of my emotional reserves if I was going to survive what was coming my way.

I left the office and headed back downstairs. Kyle was still sleeping, but he wasn't shivering anymore. I warmed up the hot packs again and slid them under the covers.

I considered climbing back in bed with Kyle, but there wasn't any desire behind the thought. I just felt like I was supposed to be under the covers with him because that was what I was used to doing.

I couldn't do it though, not without making things worse with Jace, and I didn't want that—just like I didn't want to lead Kyle on any more than I already had. I didn't understand how I'd gotten here. I'd always thought I was a good person; I wasn't so sure anymore.

There was an element of risk to leaving Kyle there by himself, but I couldn't bring myself to stay there with him, watching him sleep. I couldn't stand the idea of being there when he woke up and having to face him.

Just going upstairs and watching a movie didn't seem appropriate. Besides, I wouldn't be able to concentrate on it even if I'd wanted to. Instead, I ended up going back out to the stairwell and heading down.

I'd had vague thoughts of going to the garden and harvesting the ingredients for one last meal with Kyle, but that didn't seem right. It was playing house with him that had helped put me in my current mess. Taking care of him, pretending he was truly mine, even just for a little bit, was just going to make things harder.

Instead, I ended up in his workshop. I couldn't have said for sure what drew me into that room with its shimmering ward and its countless blackboards, but something made me push the door open and sit down on one of the hard metal chairs.

I looked at Kyle's egg-shaped creation, the device that sped us along at twice the speed of the rest of the world, but I didn't know how to plumb the depths of its secrets any more than I knew how to read the equations on Kyle's blackboards.

Instead of doing anything productive, I just sat there and stared at the equations and wished that I knew why those last two boards looked so wrong to me.

I lost track of time. It might have been two hours or it might have been four, but in the end it didn't matter. Enough time had passed that I needed to go back upstairs and wake Kyle up so that I could ask him the best way for Jace and Kat to find us.

I stood to go, but instead of walking over to the door, I went over to the second-to-last blackboard, one of the two that seemed so wrong. I smeared out two of the letters, swapping them, and then changed four of the signs scattered around the board.

As soon as I realized what I'd done I started freaking out. I reached up, intending on changing it back, hoping that I would be able to remember everything I'd changed, but my smudges looked just like Kyle's smudges.

It wasn't going to be enough, but I could at least change the two letters back. Hand shaking, I reached back up to make the correction, only Kyle had somehow managed to enter the room without me hearing him.

"Wait. Stop."

"I'm sorry, Kyle. I wasn't thinking—it just didn't look right. Please tell me you can fix it!"

He looked at the board and I couldn't read the expression that crossed his face. Despite all odds, I held onto hope right up until he shook his head.

"I can't fix it, Selene."

I turned away from him. I couldn't meet his eyes, knowing that I'd ruined countless hours of work. I expected him to lash out at me—even despite his promise.

I jumped when I felt his hand on my arm, but his touch was gentle. "You don't understand, Selene. I can't fix it because it wasn't right before, but it is now. You fixed it. You solved one of the fundamental problems that has been stopping me from progressing my research beyond its current state. *You* fixed it."

"How is that even possible? I don't know what any of this means."

"I don't know how, but you weren't working on an advanced form of time amp or a better shield or a new way of healing people. All of those rumors were just that. They were rumors so that people wouldn't realize what you were actually working on. You probably didn't even tell Jace and Kat about your actual research."

"What do you mean?"

"I mean you were trying to come up with the theoretical underpinnings that would allow you to create new artifacts. You and I were pursuing the same research and—at least in some ways—you were ahead of me."

He hurried over to the last blackboard, obviously weak, but too excited to let that stop him.

"What about this one? Do you know where I'm going wrong with this one?"

I slowly shook my head. "I'm sorry, Kyle, but I don't. I don't even know how I was able to fix the first one. I thought this was impossible."

That pulled him up short. He was just as capable of losing himself in the excitement of the moment as anyone else, but I'd just pointed him towards an even bigger mystery and he latched onto it like a pit bull.

"You're right, it doesn't make any sense. I've never heard of anyone pulling memories through a death like that. Then again, you seem to be picking up new effects much more quickly than you have any right to."

I debated not telling him the rest of the oddness we'd detected so far about me, but if he was going to be any help then he needed to know everything.

"That's not all, Kyle. When I first awakened, I got the normal crystallization of my memories and the increased vividness that comes with that, but it didn't just happen for the memories from that point forward. I nearly lost myself in a memory from before awakening. It happened to all of my memories, even stuff that I thought I'd forgotten."

Kyle stumbled over to a chair and shook his head. "That shouldn't be possible. If it was someone else, I'd suspect them of lying, of trying to waste my time by sending me down a false lead. I saw you fix my equations though..."

For several seconds he didn't say anything. "Are you sure that you really died? Maybe Jace and Kat faked your death to get Mephistoles to leave the three of you alone."

That made me laugh. "I remember growing up. We still have baby clothes at my house—in fact, I think we've still got every outfit I ever wore growing up packed away up in the attic."

"Maybe your research wasn't actually designed to let you create new artifacts. An understanding of memories is integral to creating an artifact, but maybe that was just a happy coincidence. Maybe you were researching ways to manipulate memories. Maybe you wanted to drop out of sight and knew that it would never work if you behaved like your-self."

I grabbed Kyle's arm and pulled on it to get his attention. "You're going off half-cocked. Faking my own death doesn't make any sense. It wouldn't have accomplished anything. Mephistoles didn't want me, he wanted my journals. Faking my death wouldn't have done anything to take pressure off of Jace and Kat."

Kyle grimaced slightly at my use of his brother's name. It was interesting that he hadn't reacted at all when it had been him using Jace's name.

"It wouldn't have done anything to take the pressure off, but it could explain how the two of them managed to stay one step ahead of Mephistoles for nearly two decades. Nobody expected them to last this long. Maybe you faked your death but continued to run with them until very recently so that you could take your enemies by surprise…"

"And my family? My dad and Ari, what about them? You think that I just grabbed a couple of people off of the street and wiped their memories too, implanting some kind of shared history?"

"Yes."

"That wouldn't do anything to hide my presence from any Awakened who passed by. It would have just made me a sitting duck for anyone who happened to drive through town."

"Maybe you found a way to mask your ability, a way that made it so you couldn't be detected by others of our kind."

"You're reaching, Kyle. In order for your hypothesis to work, I would have had to have made two fairly unrelated discoveries. If I knew how to shield my presence from other Awakened it would have made a lot more sense for me to just sneak up on them and assassinate everyone who gave us any problems."

"That's a fair point. I'm out of ideas though. I don't know how you're doing this."

"Yeah, that makes two of us."

Chapter 23

Kyle wanted to feed me one last meal, but I refused to let him. He was stronger than he'd been up to that point, but still too weak to waste his strength on pointless tasks. Instead I convinced him to let me help him up to his office so that he could show me how to work the video feeds and provide me with written directions that would get Jace and Kat from the road to the Lost City as quickly as possible.

I checked the feeds and confirmed that Fenrir and the other two hadn't managed to bring down the third ward yet. Ironically, having the other two fae around seemed to be slowing down Fenrir's progress. He wasn't as willing to push himself as hard now that there was a chance one of the other two might attack him while he was incapacitated.

Then I called Kat and gave her the directions to the third ward. The trickiest part was going to be making sure that we all attacked at the same time. I promised to go out to the third ward and wait just behind it so that I could follow Fenrir if he made a break towards the surface in an attempt to kill my friends before they could link up with me.

By the time my call to Kat was done, Kyle was shivering again. I tried to help him back down to his bedroom so he'd be close to the bath in case his fever kicked back up, but he wordlessly pushed my hands away and started down the stairs by himself.

I watched him slowly make his way down to the next level and tried to come up with something to say, something that would make everything right. In the end I just stood there, unable to speak. Kyle turned back and looked at me just before he disappeared, but it was like there was a stranger looking out of his eyes. He'd already started distancing himself from me.

I understood that he didn't want to get hurt. I even recognized that I didn't have any room to complain—not when I was the one who couldn't seem to make up her mind—but that didn't make it any easier. There was so much potential good inside of Kyle, but he'd spent centuries pushing that part of himself away.

I waited until I heard his door clang shut and then I started upstairs to the kitchen. My shoes hadn't taken the kind of time-amped punishment that Kyle had dealt to his, but they still looked like they'd been through a small war. Unlike

Kyle, I didn't have spares stockpiled, but I knew I needed to do something.

I ate a couple of oranges as I tried to come up with a solution. I ended up finding some duct tape in one of the kitchen drawers and used it to reinforce my shoes. I didn't know how well the tape would grip on the rock floor of the city, so I left big chunks of exposed sole as I wrapped the tape the short way around my feet. The result was ugly as sin, and I was going to have to remember to stay on the balls of my feet, but I was hopeful that it would let my shoes last for at least one more fight.

It took me another half an hour to dig up a flashlight and a lantern. I was getting antsy about the amount of time I'd been stuck waiting inside of the bunker, but by my calculations I still had plenty of time before Jace and Kat would be arriving. Besides, there wasn't any way I was going back out in the darkness by myself without something to help me find my way to the third ward.

I experimented with the lantern until I was able to get it working and then grabbed it, the backup flashlight, and a small can of extra fuel before heading over to the outside door. Both of the swords I'd left at the door when I'd brought Kyle back to the bunker were waiting for me, and I was faced with a tough decision.

Taking my sword wasn't a problem. I could leave it just inside the third ward after the battle was over, and even if that didn't work out, Kyle wouldn't care. Taking Excalibur would be a different matter entirely.

It was sitting there in its leather scabbard, beckoning to me, a powerful artifact that would allow me to keep hold of my memories, an artifact that could make all of the difference between winning or losing.

There wasn't anything to stop me from taking it, either. Kyle was downstairs, locked behind his bedroom door, barely strong enough to shuffle up one or two sets of stairs. I could grab it right then and there, and by the time he wondered what had happened to it I would be too far away for him to stop me before I made it to the third ward.

I told myself that it was just temporary, that I would just borrow it, use it to fight Fenrir, and then leave it waiting for Kyle just inside the third ward. Looked at in that light, it felt no different than what I was doing with the lantern, but I knew that wasn't the case.

The lantern could be replaced with an infinitesimal fraction of the proceeds from selling just one bar of platinum. Excalibur was one of a kind and if something happened to me during the fight Kyle would never get it back.

There was nothing stopping me from taking it other than the knowledge that doing so would be wrong—that and the fact that Kyle would never forgive me for taking Excalibur. If I was really going to take it then I should just walk downstairs and use it to slit Kyle's throat.

If I took it, then he and I would forever be at odds. One of us would have to die if I betrayed him like that, and I wasn't willing to do that, not even for my dad—he wouldn't have wanted me to.

I reached down and stroked Excalibur's hilt, marveling at how warm it felt despite having been sitting there for the last two days.

"You're a magnificent weapon. I wish I could take you with me, but you're not mine to take. Please take care of him. Even if he and I don't end up together—even if I end up a lonely old woman with no friends at all—it will be a little easier knowing that he's got you to help keep him safe."

I put my flashlight into my back pocket, slid the hilt of my sword through the handle of the fuel can, and then balanced my sword across my shoulders. Two minutes later, even the door to the bunker had slipped away into the darkness like it had never existed.

I half expected to get lost on my way to the third ward, but it turned out that I had a better sense of direction than I'd given myself credit for. A surge of fear crashed through me as I crossed the fourth ward and realized there was a chance that Fenrir had taken down the third ward since I'd last checked on it, but there was nothing to do but keep walking and hope for the best.

Somewhere between the fourth and third wards the time-bending effect disappeared. It had been keeping pace with me up until then, moving with the same erratic fits and starts. Honestly, I was surprised that it stayed with me as long as it did. It was programmed to surround Kyle. There was no reason to think that it would stick with me for long enough to fight Fenrir, but as I stepped right up to the edge of the vivid colors that marked the edge of the effect, I felt a sense of loss. I wasn't just crossing a line, I was returning to a different state of existence, a state that was lacking some of the magic that had defined my time with Kyle.

I wasn't just more exposed, I was losing out on something unique, something nobody else in the entire world was capable of recreating.

I'd known the odds of Fenrir taking down the ward while I was traveling out to it were small, but it was still a relief when I made it to the spot where we'd fought the last time. The lantern cast a wide circle of light at my feet that revealed pools of dried blood, and it wasn't until I looked around that I realized just how much blood had been lost in that last fight.

Some of it was Fenrir's, but most of it was Kyle's. It was amazing that he'd survived for long enough to heal himself. I set the lantern down and pumped it up some more before turning and meeting Fenrir's eyes.

"Here to tell me that your boy toy is dead?"

"No, I'm just here to watch."

Fenrir laughed, a rumbling, coughing sound. "That might have worked before my associates arrived, but only if it was Kyle standing in your place. You won't manage to slow me appreciably. If you have any brains you'll just cross over to this side of the ward and let me kill you now in the hopes that I'll make it fast."

"I didn't come here for mercy. I just came to watch. If you're right and it's only a matter of time before I die, then before I go I'll at least have the pleasure of watching you suffer."

The words had come from somewhere else, somewhere darker, a place I hadn't realized existed inside of me. It was true. I was looking forward to seeing Fenrir howl in agony as he tried to break through the ward. It was wrong on several levels, but it was also exactly the right thing to say if I wanted to piss off Fenrir. The big wolf threw himself into the ward with a force that had been lacking on the last several attempts I'd seen on the video feed.

It was an obvious bid to drain the last of the ward's power in one quick burst, but luckily for me it failed. Instead of crashing through and ripping out my throat, Fenrir was thrown back into the rock wall with enough force that I heard bones snap.

I looked over to the horse, the pooka, while Fenrir shook and screamed on the floor. "You know you could take him down right now and then run away as one of the few fae to have disembodied the mighty Fenrir?"

Fenrir struggled to his feet, bones popping back into place as he used some of his stored power to force an immediate healing.

"They wouldn't dare. I would hunt them to the ends of the world and extinguish them."

I forced myself not to smile. My understanding was that the only way for Fenrir to absorb more energy from the ward than he lost was to press up against it a little bit at a time. Displays like he'd just demonstrated resulted in a net loss in vitality, and that was even more the case when he forced his body to heal so rapidly.

"Really? For one little disembodying? Just in the last few days Kyle and I have disembodied you twice. Your poison has done a real number on Kyle, but he'll be back. Maybe you'll kill us in the end, but it will be interesting to see how many more times we're able to disembody you before that happens. Personally I think you'd have to let them go. Kyle and I are the more dangerous threats."

"Unlike you, I'm truly immortal. I know things that you puny gods have long forgotten. I have all the time in the world. Eventually all slights will be repaid."

I shrugged. "Maybe. Then again, I'm sure you have enemies inside of the Unseelie Court. Some of them are no doubt as strong as you. All it would take is for Kyle or me to get hold of one of those enemies and let them know that you've been disembodied twice recently and bled out like nobody's business. I'm sure they would wait until the last possible second. They'd want you to spend yourself against Kyle and me before they make an appearance, but eventually they would show."

"You're bluffing. Someone like that would just continue my efforts here after I was gone."

"Maybe. Then again, if they thought that they had a chance of extinguishing you, it's entirely possible that they'd hang around and just...what is the term? Farm? Yes, that's it, they might just stay around and farm you. Besides, if you're right and it's really just a matter of time before Kyle and I are dead, what do we have to lose?"

Fenrir looked back and forth and I almost felt like I could read his mind. If he left the ward to go watch for a new arrival then he'd be leaving the other two fae alone to face the worst that Kyle and I were capable of. He didn't particularly care about either of the other two, but if he wasn't here pushing up against the ward then it would never come down.

Then again, if he sent the other two out to check for his biggest rivals in the Unseelie court then he would be letting them out of his sight and it was entirely possible that they would decide to run to one of his enemies and sell him out. It was a risky play, but if they really thought that Fenrir's star was starting to fall then there was something to be said for seeking protection from one of the other powers in the court.

In his own way Fenrir was just as trapped as I was. Once Mephistoles had left him and he'd been forced to bring in backup, he'd stepped onto a path that demanded he take Kyle and me down. It meant that he was desperate. Not as desperate as we were, but desperate all the same.

Desperate people eventually make big mistakes.

I wondered how much of that Kyle had foreseen. He'd definitely known that he was pushing Mephistoles out, but had he known that he was going to put Fenrir into such a tricky spot? It was possible. Kyle understood the way things worked much better than I did.

"You're bluffing. Run along and hide behind the other ward I can feel on the far side of this one."

"No, thanks, I'm going to sit here and watch."

Fenrir pushed up against the ward again, tinging the pool of light at my side an electric blue, but he was much more cautious this time. He wanted me dead, but he was apparently going to do it the slow way and try to gain as much power from the process as possible.

To say that I sat there and watched him wouldn't have been exactly accurate. I sat there, but I spent most of the time with my eyes closed. Watching Fenrir try to bring the ward down would have just made me jumpy.

Instead, I tried to practice the new default emotion that I'd started trying to rewire myself for back before Fenrir had chased me the first time. I was starting to understand Kat's frustration with me. I'd already built up such an incredible emotional reserve when it came to anger that it seemed wasteful not to build on it.

Everything Kat had told me was true, but there were things that I hadn't properly appreciated back in the day. I'd been so focused on the fact that I only had seventeen years of memories and the disadvantage that put me under, that I hadn't realized that most of the time it was the strength of my emotions that was going to be the limiting factor.

I'd fallen into the same trap so many other people did. It was easy to hear about some extreme example and think that was what I should be aiming for, but the truth was that those kinds of events were passed around and talked about precisely because they were so unique.

Kat had told me about instances when people had burned themselves dry over the course of just an hour or two, and I'd somehow thought that was normal. I'd thought that memories were the real key to power. It wasn't until I'd seen just how scared everyone was of Mephistoles that it had really started sinking in.

The smart thing would be for me to stop screwing around with my default emotion. I should be embracing the anger and stoking it even higher, but the thought of doing that scared me. I'd seen at least one of the potential results of walking down that path.

Kyle had wanted to be with me even back when he'd first brought me here to his bunker. He'd probably even wanted to be with me right after he'd burned away all of his memories. Despite that, the sheer strength of his anger kept getting in the way. I didn't want that any more than I wanted to spend all of my time afraid of what would happen next.

If I had to choose between a long life full of anger and fear or a short life filled with happiness, I would pick the short life option. Maybe not every time—certainly not the last time—but that was what I was picking this time.

I sat there and practiced summoning the pure, uncomplicated joy I'd felt back when Jace had first rescued me from Sandra. It should have been hard—it was, really—but it wasn't as hard as I'd been expecting it to be. I just focused on all of the reasons I had to be happy.

I had Kat's friendship, a girl—a woman, really—who was willing to risk Jace being mad at her if that was what it took to save me and give my dad a chance at surviving the mess we were in.

I had Ari. She wasn't the best sister anyone had ever had, but in her own way she cared about me as much as I cared about her.

Over the last week I'd had the chance to meet not just one, but two guys who wanted me for who I was on the inside even more than what I looked like on the outside. That would have been unexpected enough all by itself, but they were both amazing in ways that I had a hard time explaining.

I might have messed things up with both of them, but at least I'd always know that they'd both wanted me right up until I'd torpedoed my chances with them.

That was all plenty of reason to be happy, but somewhere along the way I'd rediscovered something I never should have lost sight of. I had an amazing father, one who put everything he had into taking care of us, one who loved me no matter what I did, one who wanted the best for me, even if it meant that his life wasn't as good as he would have liked it to be.

Even if I died in the next few hours, I would die having experienced things most people never experienced, having loved in ways that most people never loved. That was something to be happy about.

Happiness settled over me with a comforting weight. It didn't push me to act like anger always did, happiness was an emotion that was pleased to just sit and reflect. For the first time in my life I felt like I was part of something bigger.

It wasn't the moment of oneness that people referred to when they talked about enlightenment, but I felt a definite sense of clicking into place with the universe around me.

Fenrir brushed up against the ward again and the crackle of discharging power filled the air, but this time I didn't open my eyes. I could feel something—no, two somethings—approaching. Jace and Kat were on their way.

They were keeping their augmentations light to avoid burning themselves out before arriving, but even so they were moving with inhuman speed.

I tried to guess how long it would take for them to reach me, but I didn't have enough experience to judge it correctly. I knew that I would be giving up some of the element of surprise by doing so, but I stood up regardless and drew my sword.

"Ready to run back to your lair with your tail between your legs, little one?"

I shook my head. "There are some places you just can't go back to, Fenrir."

I saw a glow approaching from the direction of the first two wards and took a deep breath as I reached for the heartbeat of this place.

It was a combination of a quiet hiss from the lantern and the slow breathing of my enemies, but it was there and I put all of the pieces in place for a time amp. The light dimmed slightly, and then Jace and Kat shot out of the darkness.

I dropped my effects into place and shot across the ward, moving at four times normal speed with the point of my sword leading the way. Circumstances couldn't have been better. My standing and drawing my sword had made the fae focus on me, which meant that Jace and Kat had taken our enemies completely by surprise.

I caught only flashes of motion as the tip of my sword took the flying monkey snake through the chest. It wasn't just that Jace and Kat were moving faster than I was—they were—it was also the fact that even as I stabbed the smallest fae I had to dodge to one side to avoid a charge from the pooka.

Jace was wielding a massive ax with both hands like it was nothing more than a child's toy while Kat had a long spear with a crosspiece at the top. As fast as they were moving they should have been able to strike Fenrir down with the first pass, but something—maybe a change in my expression—warned him at the last moment.

Fenrir shot forward a split second later and a blow from Jace's ax that should have taken Fenrir's head off instead sank deep into his ribs. For a normal animal, even one as big as Fenrir, that would have still been enough to end the fight, but Fenrir apparently hadn't lost any of his unnatural vitality. He spun around and snapped at Jace with a speed that was still hard to believe coming from something so big.

Jace threw himself backwards—leaving his ax embedded in Fenrir's side—but his efforts wouldn't have been enough if Kat hadn't stepped forward and jammed her spear into the joint between Fenrir's neck and shoulder. I didn't expect Kat's attack to do much more than barely slow Fenrir, but as soon as her weapon sank home she jammed her foot onto her end of the spear, pushing it down against the textured rock floor.

It was like watching the medieval version of some extreme sport. The floor wasn't completely smooth, but it was smooth enough that Kat's spear went skipping across the rock with her riding it like it was some kind of wild animal.

I thought Kat was dead in that instant. Her spear was still stuck in Fenrir, but as soon as she lost her balance he would trample her. A split second later the butt of her spear hit the wall behind her and Fenrir slid down the spear until he hit the crosspiece.

I would have said that nothing so slender, no metal known to man, could withstand the stress of trying to stop the better part of two tons of rampaging wolf moving at more than thirty miles per hour. I would have been mostly right.

Fenrir was picked up off of the ground and hurled towards the ceiling with an abruptness that was hard to believe. A split second later he slammed into the ceiling with enough force that I half expected him to bring the roof down on us. The shaft of Kat's spear bent, but it managed to keep Kat from being crushed.

All of that had happened in the blink of an eye. My sword was out of position, so I was forced to just jump to one side as the pooka blasted past me. I nearly wasn't fast enough. Despite my best efforts, the large horse-like fairy caught me with one shoulder and sent me reeling backwards.

I windmilled my free arm, trying to keep my balance as Jace unsheathed a sword from its position on his back and sprang forward. I managed to get my sword around so the point was directed at the pooka as it came back towards me again.

I knew I was being stupid, knew that giving my little corner of the fight anything less than my full attention was asking to be killed, but I couldn't help trying to watch out of the corner of my eye. These were my friends, people who were in danger solely in an effort to save me.

The pooka reared up, lashing out at me with its front legs, legs that had long, deadly claws. I knocked its right leg to one side, hands smarting from the force of a blow that did little more than scratch the fairy, and then charged forward, slashing at its stomach as I went.

Jace and Kat had done so well up until now that I half expected them to be on their way over to help me finish off the horse, but as I dodged back towards the center of the open space I realized that Fenrir hadn't just fallen straight back down. The force of his charge combined with the bend in the spear had sent him off to the right, and Kat's spear had caught her as Fenrir had fallen.

She was conscious and still had hold of her spear, but it definitely looked like her left leg had been broken. Fenrir rolled back up onto his feet and whipped his head around. The spear was in too deep to fall out easily, and Kat's amped hold on it was too strong for him to tear the shaft free of her hands. Instead she was flung across the floor, body dragging along behind the shaft of the spear.

Fenrir had turned her body into a weapon, but Jace easily jumped over her and his sword licked out aiming for the wolf's eyes. I had a split second in which to decide. Our situation was too terrible for us to continue on like we'd been doing.

I knew I was going to have to burn a peak memory, was going to have to generate an attack strong enough to make a real difference, but I chose to hit the pooka with my sun lance rather than aiming it at Fenrir.

I reached for my memories with the kind of desperate need I'd only felt twice before and the heat that awoke inside of me in response was like being thrown into a blast furnace. An instant later a bolt of liquid golden fire erupted from my hand and struck the pooka.

It felt like my soul was being pushed out through the center of my forehead, but the results were spectacular. My sun lance bored all the way through the black horse and hit the rock wall on the other side. The pooka dropped to the ground, instantly dead, and I turned around just in time to see Fenrir whip the free end of the spear around with such force that Kat lost her grip on it.

As I ran forward, intending on pulling her back out of the way, the butt of the spear hit Jace and knocked him into a wall with enough force that I half expected his arm to snap. Jace bounced off of the wall and shook his head as though trying to get the world to stop spinning, but I could already tell that he'd lost the initiative.

I made as though to help Kat, but she waved me towards Jace. "Help him! I just need a second to heal my leg."

I charged into Fenrir, leading with the tip of my sword again, all of my weight focused behind its deadly point, but I'd misjudged Fenrir's situational awareness. I bought Jace just enough time to get out of Fenrir's range, but Fenrir spun around and slammed his shoulder into me a split-second before my sword would have otherwise struck home.

I'd never been hit that hard before at any point in my life, and I suddenly realized that super-hard bones wouldn't do anything to protect my brain from injury. My vision swam, and for a second I thought I was going to throw up.

A loud clang brought my head around and I opened my eyes to see Jace's sword bounce off the wall after ricocheting off of the floor. Fenrir had Jace trapped in the corner and it was obvious to me that he was hoping to be able to play with Jace for a while before killing him.

I tried to reach for the emotions I would need to burn another peak memory, but the blow to my head had left me feeling like my emotions were wrapped in gauze. Jace conjured up a sun lance of his own, but Fenrir dodged aside at the last instant and I knew that all the attack had done was restore some of the strength the big wolf had lost recently.

Jace yelled and charged forward. Fenrir sprang toward my boyfriend, but then all of a sudden someone else barreled into Fenrir from the side.

It was a woman, one who was about my size, with short, beautiful dark hair and skin that had an odd shimmer to it in the artificial light from the lantern. I thought for a minute that hitting my head so hard had made me hallucinate. There didn't seem to be any other explanation.

The newcomer couldn't weigh more than a hundred and thirty pounds, but somehow she collided with Fenrir hard enough to knock the two-ton wolf sprawling end for end. I was still trying to get my feet to work, trying to blink my eyes clear of this impossible scene, but she'd grabbed Jace's ax from where it was buried in Fenrir's side as he'd gone cartwheeling away from her, and as Fenrir bounced off of the wall and came around snarling she hit him across the face with the haft of the ax hard enough that the metal deformed.

Jace sped past me, slowing just long enough to grab his sword, and then he headed straight towards the fight. I heard Kat moving behind me as she came out of the near trance required for her to heal her leg, but it was obvious to me that she wasn't going to make it over in time to help out—the fight was progressing too quickly.

The blow from the ax handle had staggered Fenrir, but he still shifted back to the offensive fast enough that the newcomer had to jump to one side. Fenrir spun and snapped at her. I could see that he was trying to back her into a corner, but she was just as fast as he was, and Jace was close enough that Fenrir had to worry about him too.

Jace slashed at Fenrir—an attack designed more to wound than to kill, but one that Fenrir had to honor. As the massive dire wolf shifted his weight around to the side, the woman stepped in and slammed her ax into Fenrir with enough force to sink the ax more than two feet into his back.

A few seconds later Fenrir was nothing more than a corpse that was melting into the air, and Bethany was standing on my sternum. "Sorry, I would have arrived sooner, but I'm not even close to being in Fenrir's league. Besides, if he'd disembodied me that probably would have been game over."

Jace arrived at my side a second later and the warm healing energy coming from his hands was the most welcome thing I could have imagined in that moment.

"Just hold still for a moment, Selene. I'll have you back on your feet before you know it."

Once Jace was done, he and Kat both helped me to my feet and we walked over to the woman who was kneeling on the stone floor with her eyes closed.

I wasn't sure exactly what I was supposed to do. She hadn't acknowledged any of us, but based on the way that Jace and Kat were behaving, this woman was extremely important.

I took the opportunity to get a better look at her. She was beautiful in a way that I could never hope to manage. Her face and hair were flawless, and she had the willowy build of a runway model, but all of that paled in comparison to her skin.

She wasn't just pale like I was. It actually looked like underneath her skin she was nothing more than a being of pure light. Even as I thought that, I felt a growing frustration over the fact that I wasn't doing her justice.

She wasn't radiating light or anything as gaudy as that, she just seemed like there was something more to her, something just under the surface, something that put her completely out of my league.

"You did well bringing me here, little sister."

I thought for a moment that she was addressing Kat, or failing that, me. It turned out I was wrong on both counts. She was talking to Bethany, who stood up to her full three inches of height and all but saluted.

"Thank you, my liege. I knew that Selene and Kyle had been fighting Fenrir, so it was reasonable to assume that they would have weakened him. When Jace and Kat promised to enter the battle as well, it seemed too good an opportunity to pass up."

"Indeed. And none of that had anything to do with the fact that you were worried about your friends?"

"Would you have come if I'd told you that I needed your help in a hopeless fight that we couldn't possibly win? Punish me if you must, but my first loyalty is to Genevieve and my second loyalty is to Selene. The Seelie Court is a distant fifth or sixth for me right now."

The woman opened her eyes and looked at me for several seconds before turning her stare to Bethany.

"You might be surprised at what I would be willing to do. That is water under the bridge now though. I will spend a few more minutes here absorbing as much of Fenrir's lost strength as possible, and then I will pursue him. I doubt that I'll manage to close with him again—he's much too wily to be caught easily, but I'll chase him halfway back to the Unseelie Court on the chance that I might be able to bring him to bay again."

The beautiful, unearthly woman looked at me again. "I am the Lady. You've changed from your last incarnation, Selene."

I bit off a hysterical laugh. "It seems like people have done nothing over the last few days but tell me how *unchanged* I am."

"I'm sure they are right when it comes to the superficial, but in one very important way you seem to be changing, or at least making the effort. I'm sure it must be hard not to just default back to rage all of the time."

It took me a second to find my voice. "Did Bethany tell you that?"

"No. Bethany can tell whether you're defaulting to anger or...something else, but that is simply because she can only feed off of effects powered by a certain kind of emotion. I, on the other hand, have amassed the power required to know what emotions are feeding me. Not many would make the choice you're making."

"I'm not perfect at it. If I don't have enough emotional reserve using a positive emotion I default back to anger, but I'm trying."

A sound from behind us brought everyone around. It was Kyle. He looked like he'd been through hell and back—the trip from the bunker had obviously taken a tremendous amount out of him, but he was there standing behind the third ward with Excalibur at his hip and a white-bound journal under his arm.

I opened my mouth to tell him that he shouldn't be out here where he couldn't regulate his body temperature, but I couldn't get the words out. I hadn't expected to have Jace and Kyle in the same spot at the same time—especially not before I'd had a chance to tell Jace what had happened.

Kyle's eyes were practically burning a hole into Jace, and when I looked over at Jace I realized that he knew. I couldn't have said for sure how he knew, or even how I knew that he knew, but he was aware that I'd kissed Kyle.

Kat looked like she wanted to say something to defuse the situation, but she was as stumped there as I was. The silence stretched out for nearly a minute before the Lady walked over to the very edge of the ward and captured Kyle's gaze with her own.

"I was not aware that you had taken possession of Excalibur."

"It's a relatively recent development."

She smiled, but the expression didn't make it to her eyes. "Every development is recent to someone like me. Even my decision to give that blade to Arthur feels like it happened just yesterday. How did you get your hands on it?"

"I played to the previous owner's weaknesses."

"That sword is mine, and always will be. Give it to me and you will have my thanks both for returning the sword to me and for saving me the work of killing Isepeth myself."

"If you want to trade for Excalibur then give me something of equal value. If all you've come to do is threaten and demand then you can leave. I'm not interested in listening to more of the same bluster Fenrir is so good at."

"I'm not Fenrir. I could have my lieutenants here within a few hours and we could bring your wards down within a few days. The Seelie Court isn't plagued by the internal dissent that cripples our darker brethren. If I decide that you'll die before the week is out, it will be so."

I knew what Kyle had been through over the last two days. Even being locked away in the bunker while I'd been waiting for Jace and Kat to arrive hadn't bought him more than an hour or two more to recover. He had to be at the very end of his endurance, had to be standing there solely through willpower and pride, but at that moment I almost believed that he was still the same demigod who had chased Mephistoles off and then proceeded to fight Fenrir to a standstill three times in two days.

He looked indomitable. He looked like one of the gods we'd once believed ourselves to be.

"You don't have the infighting that charac- terizes the Unseelie Court, but they have you outnumbered three to one. That's the little secret that you all try so hard not to think about. It's much easier for people to be bad than it is for them to be good. It's true for humans, and it's true for we Awakened. Your court may be more united, but your numbers are only barely sufficient to keep up with your commitments. You're locked in an eternal, grinding war where nobody ever really dies. If you pulled your most trusted servants in to help you take down my defenses you would win here, but you'd lose everywhere else. Gains that you've spent the last three hundred years trying to consolidate would be wiped out in a matter of days."

"Please stop fighting!"

It took me a second to realize that it had been me who'd screamed.

"Kyle, stop antagonizing her. You have nothing to win and everything to lose." I turned to the Lady and bowed my head to show her the respect that everyone but Kyle seemed to think she deserved. "Please don't do this. Kyle saved Kat and me from Fenrir and has been responsible for disembodying that monster twice in the last few days. Kyle has his share of problems, but he's not the enemy. Please let him keep the sword and come help us fight Mephistoles."

She didn't look at me—at least not at first. Instead she placed her hand millimeters from Kyle's ward and a finger-sized stream of crackling energy discharged from the ward into her hand.

"I don't have to rely on the same kind of brute-force methods that Fenrir employs. If Jace and Kat are willing to stay here and watch my back I won't even have to call in my lieutenants."

Kyle opened his mouth, but she cut him off with a look that was full of such terrible majesty that all of us took a step back.

"You're right that my presence here puts other accomplishments at risk, and Selene is right that Fenrir and his kind are my true enemies, but if Selene is wrong about you, I will come back here and take away your life. The only thing that has stopped me from doing so before now is that you're not as dark as some and I worry about what you'd come back as. Don't make me regret my leniency."

The energy discharging from Kyle's ward had been slowly growing the entire time that the Lady was talking. By the time she was done, it had engulfed her arm almost all the way up to her shoulder, a radiant, blue cocoon that should have vaporized her entire arm, but which didn't seem to be harming her in the slightest.

She turned away from Kyle and started towards the surface, holding her arm out away from her body while she walked. I started to go after her, but before I could take my first step, I remembered that Kyle was holding what I suspected was my journal.

"Kyle, is that my journal?"

"Yes."

"May I have it? I don't read French yet, but I'll learn. I'd like to know what else is in there."

"Sure, just come through the ward."

"Don't do it! You can't trust him, Selene. He's a snake."

Jace's voice was anguished in a way that I'd never heard out of him before. I wanted to disagree, wanted to tell him that Kyle wouldn't hurt me or hold me there against my will, but there was something in Kyle's eyes that I couldn't read. It almost felt like Kyle himself wasn't sure whether he would do those things.

I looked at him and held out my hand, stopping a few inches away from the ward even though I knew it wouldn't hurt me. "Can you just hand it through?"

"After everything you still don't trust me."

"It's hard to trust you right now when I can see that you're not entirely sure what you're going to do."

"I could force the issue. I could make you choose here and now."

That last bit was said so quietly I was almost certain that Jace hadn't heard it, but I still wanted to crawl under a rock and hide for the next thousand years. I didn't run away though because I had people who depended on me.

"If you force a choice right now the choice will go against you, Kyle. Apart from everything else there's still the matter of my dad being Mephistoles' prisoner. I have to get him out, and you're not in any condition to help with that."

"I could be by the time we arrive."

"Then come help us. It sounds like it's going to be touch and go with just Kat, Jace and me since Mephistoles has someone helping him. We could really use you."

"I will not assist my brother, not if my life depended on it."

"You wouldn't be helping Jace, you would be helping me."

Kyle gritted his teeth. "There is no difference. I will not help him, not even indirectly."

"You're lucky he doesn't live by the same rule or you and I would both be nothing but rotting corpses inside of your bunker."

I turned and walked away without looking back. I cursed myself all of the way back out to the surface. I'd made the wrong choice in trying for Kyle's help—I would have been much better off trying for the Lady's assistance.

I expected Jace to tear into me at any moment, but he just led the way through nearly a mile of dark spaces and twisty hallways illuminated only by the pair of lights floating above my friends' shoulders.

I kept trying to come up with a way to break the awkward silence, but nothing seemed appropriate—especially not with Kat walking between Jace and I like she was, especially not when every second might count when it came to getting back to free my dad.

When we finally slipped around a pair of large rocks and out into the sunlight I was astonished at just how bright the natural light was. I was squinting, but it was still so bad that I could barely make anything out.

Bethany had settled back onto my shoulder, but even she seemed to be having a hard time dealing with the sunlight. She only managed a warning a split second before I crashed into what turned out to be the Lady.

I should have at least knocked her off balance, but it was like bouncing off a warm, soft boulder. She grabbed me, steadying me before I could fall.

"You should hold still until your eyes have finished adjusting."

"Thank you. I'm sorry for running into you."

"It's fine, all of us older, more powerful fairies are capable of adjusting our weight. Unless I'm making a special effort to lighten myself I weigh in at just over a ton. In an emergency I can double that. You would have had to hit me a lot harder than that to cause me any real problems."

"I guess that explains how you were able to knock Fenrir around like that. It makes a lot of sense, but you've got to be the only female in the world willing to publicly admit to her real weight."

It wasn't exactly the most appropriate thing to have said—she was the queen of the Seelie Court, or at least the next best thing to a queen—but it had just popped out. If she'd taken issue with my comment I would have blamed it on the sunlight or the fact that I'd been in several fights for my life since I'd found out that I was one of the Awakened, but she didn't seem to mind.

That was probably good; I didn't really want to lie to her. The truth was that there was more to it than just those things. When she'd touched me it had sent a surge through me that I didn't know how to interpret. It wasn't sexual like what I felt with Jace or Kyle, but it seemed to shoot through me and revitalize everything it touched. She was better than caffeine by a long shot.

"I'm far too old to care what any males—fae, human or otherwise—might think of my figure. Besides, weight doesn't mean quite the same thing in my culture as it does in yours. In our culture, it is a thing to be celebrated. It represents power, it helps keep you safe."

"Wow, there is so much about the world that I didn't even realize I didn't know. I look forward to the day when I know everything there is to know."

"As one of the Awakened you should have more care with your words. Unlike the humans who are so fond of such hyperbole, you actually could eventually achieve that goal. At least when it comes to knowing most everything worth knowing. I'm not sure that the prize would be worth the effort though."

My eyes had cleared enough to see the Lady. She was even more incredible-looking out in natural light, but I'd more or less expected that. I wasn't expecting for her to be looking at me with another expression that I couldn't even begin to interpret.

"You have a question, Selene. Go ahead and ask it."

"Will you come help us defeat Mephistoles? We could really use you. I'm not sure that we can do it without you."

"I'm sorry, Selene. I wish I could, but there are other considerations. The only thing I can guarantee right now is that I'll keep Fenrir occupied for at least the next few hours."

"There were two other fae here earlier too. You'll have to worry about them as well..."

"I know. Jace informed me of their presence, but they are minor powers and Fenrir will reform hours before they will. Unless another member of the dark court comes here looking for Fenrir or me for some reason, it will just be the two of us."

"You can beat him again?"

"Nothing is guaranteed. Fenrir has been hiding the true extent of his powers for quite a while now, but he's just suffered through three dissolutions in short order. My odds are very good. I won't be able to stay here forever, but there is a good chance that I can kill him at least once or twice before I have to leave. With a bit of luck I'll be able to kill the pooka too."

"How will you find him when he reforms?"

"I'll be able to sense him. Not exactly, and not for long, but well enough that he won't be able to hide from me. If he reforms inside of the city then he'll have to go past me to get out. If he reforms out here then I'll be able to tell that simply by his direction of travel."

"Okay, I think I understand. I wish you were coming with us, but you have things that you should be doing. I guess the proper goodbye is to wish you good hunting?"

"I doubt that you do understand, but yes, that will do."

I turned to go, but she grabbed my shoulder before I could take a step. "I wish that the world you crave was one that was possible. Once upon a time your kind and my kind worked together, but now it's nothing more than an unobtainable dream. Only the newly born can indulge in that kind of relationship."

Chapter 24

The drive back to Colorado went by much faster than I would have believed possible, but it still seemed like it took forever. We were riding in a silver Mercedes and Kat kept the accelerator all the way to the floor for nearly the entire trip.

I'd half been expecting her to use some kind of advanced effect to make us not show up on radar, but she did it the old-fashioned way—with a radar detector and white knuckles. Apparently she didn't feel like she could spare the emotional reserves to maintain any kind of effect for that period of time—not when we were going to be fighting Mephistoles once we got back to Colorado.

It was awkward as all get-out, but I tried to talk to Jace while we were still on the road. It felt like the wrong move to get into everything while Kat and Bethany were there listening, but I also didn't feel right not saying anything.

Jace shut me down before I even got started.

"Now isn't the time. We can talk once your dad is okay."

"But it's not fair for you to go into that fight under false pretenses…"

"I'm not. I'm going into it because your dad is a decent guy and Kat would never let me hear the end of it if we didn't at least try to save him."

The scattered pieces of the puzzle finally clicked into place and I turned to Kat.

"You're in love with my dad!"

Kat flinched, but she didn't look away from the road. "I'm not in love with your dad—not yet, at least. I would like to get to know him better though. He's attractive, interesting and a genuinely good person. I was going to tell you earlier, but I just hadn't figured out how to bring it up. The fact that he's been captured by Mephistoles sucks on every level, but if we manage to get him out of there it will mean that he's already part of our world. That's a major bonus in a potential boyfriend."

Part of me wanted to yell that it was completely unacceptable for her to be crushing on my dad, but I kept my mouth shut. I was the last person who should be complaining about her keeping secrets from me—not considering the size of the secret I was still kind of keeping from Jace.

I was going to have to just grin and hope that everything worked out between the two of them. I wasn't ready for my mom to be replaced—her death still felt like it had happened just yesterday, but my dad could do a lot worse than Kat and they'd both been lonely for far too long.

I split the remaining time between looking over at Kat and back at Jace, but nobody said anything else for the entire rest of the drive. It was hard to believe, but we'd each managed to do something to alienate the other two. That wasn't quite right, I wasn't pissed at Jace, and Kat probably wasn't pissed at him either, but there was still something unresolved between all of us.

It wasn't the kind of team that anyone in their right mind would be taking up against two Awakened demigods, but none of us felt like we had any choice but to try.

We pulled into Jace and Kat's garage half an hour before Mephistoles' deadline. Based on the lack of visible damage to the house there was a reasonable chance that Mephistoles hadn't ransacked the place, but I still walked in half expecting for the inside of the house to be in tatters. It was a relief to see that wasn't the case.

I'd only been to Jace's house a couple of times, but it still felt like home in a way that no place other than my actual home ever had. I'd always felt safe and wanted there, and that was a lot more valuable than I'd ever realized prior to this.

"Jace, I really want to talk to you. I know you don't want to talk to me, and I'll respect that if you're determined to keep me at arm's length, but I hate the thought of going into a fight where one or both of us might be killed without you knowing everything."

I was pretty sure Kat thought I was crazy, but that didn't matter. I refused to tear my eyes away from Jace.

"Kat, can you call Mephistoles and then bring the research journals up? They need to go in a fireproof vault like we talked about."

"Yeah, I can do that, but don't take too long or he'll start the party off without us."

Kat already had her cellphone out as she walked past us. Jace waited until she disappeared into the massive pantry and then pointed towards the living room. "You want to talk? Let's talk."

"Isn't she going to be coming out in a second?"

"No, the pantry is one of the few places with direct access down to the lower levels. The house was built so that you could open the other side of the pantry up and either offload into the pantry or take the food further down to the secure storage. Kat won't be back up for at least another twenty minutes by the time she checks on Ari and grabs the journals."

"Wow, the original owner really was para-noid."

"Yeah. Ironically, all of his security wouldn't stop Mephistoles for more than an hour or so without the ward that I put in place when we first moved in. It isn't as strong as I would like—not even once it's had a chance to fully stabilize, but it's far enough down that it's not detectible unless you're inside the house."

I shook my head in amazement. There was just so much I still didn't know.

"Kyle found a way to conceal stronger wards behind weaker wards. Maybe once this is over we can figure out a way to replicate what he's done and put an even stronger ward up, something that will really do the job."

Jace flinched at the sound of his brother's name, and I instantly wished I could take the words back. What the hell was I thinking?

I expected Jace to explode. He should have yelled at me and called me a slut, but he just shrugged.

"Is that even a possibility, Selene? There's no reason to put time and effort into upgrading this place if you're not going to be here. If you pick Kyle there's no reason for Kat and me to stay here. We'll go find some deep, dark hole and pull it closed behind us in the hope that we can buy ourselves another decade or two of relative safety."

"How did you know that I kissed him? Was it Kat? I begged her to let me tell you, but she refused, said that it would just ruin your focus for the fight against Fenrir. I would have rather told you myself, but if she told you then I'm still glad. I didn't want to hide anything from you."

Jace refused to meet my eyes. "She didn't have to tell me, Selene. I knew the odds. I figured if you ever met Kyle that you would have a hard time resisting him. Even after he hit you and turned against everything you believed in, it was still hard for you not to be with him."

I tried to get a word in edgewise, but Jace just kept talking. "You don't know how happy I was when you called the first time. I could hear it in your voice. I knew that you were already struggling against the attraction you were feeling for him, but you were still fighting it, I could tell that you hadn't kissed him yet. When you called Kat instead of me with your location it was all the confirmation I needed to know that you'd kissed him and maybe even…"

"No! I kissed him, but that was it. I know that was still wrong, but that was all it was."

"So you've picked him then? You just need Kat and me to help free your dad and then you'll be going back to him?"

Jace asked his question in such a lifeless, monotone voice that it was obvious he was hurting—and badly. I wanted to reach out and hug him, but I wasn't sure that I had that right anymore.

"I haven't made any choices, Jace. I wish I could say that I had, I wish that I could just tell you that I pick you, that I'd never kissed Kyle, that I'd never even been tempted, but I can't. I went into that bunker wanting nothing but a chance to spend my life with you.

"Somewhere along the way, I started wondering what life with Kyle would be like. He has one of my journals, the one that starts when we were all in London, and continues on until after he lost his memory and split away from the three of us. It's hard to explain, but that version of me told a pretty convincing story about how happy we'd been. She was desperate to make things work if Kyle ever changed enough for that to be a possibility."

Jace still refused to meet my eyes, but he was nodding. "It's true. You were inconsolable for the longest time. At one point, I thought that nothing but those memories being consumed by powering effects would let you get over him."

I'd never seen Jace so defeated. I couldn't help it any more. I grabbed his arm and pulled him around so that he had to look at me.

"You can't sit here and tell me that the last two hundred years were all like that. You and I didn't get married just out of convenience. I refuse to believe that—I wouldn't have settled for that."

"No, we were happy—extremely happy for the most part. You told me a thousand times that you were over Kyle. At first I didn't believe you, but as time went on part of me started believing. You went from just knowing that the two of you wouldn't work the way he was now to actually appreciating my differences and saying that you liked what I brought to the table. Even so, there was a part of me that wondered if you would leave me if Kyle ever came looking for you."

There was the faintest bit of life back in Jace's voice and even that small change was almost enough to make me cry.

"I know that I don't have a right to ask you to fight for us, Jace—not after what I've done—but that's what I'm trying to do. I know it sounds crazy, but it's true. I read my old journal and it sounded amazing, like I'd had everything I could have ever wanted, and that was such a powerful thing that I almost couldn't resist the idea, but I kept telling myself that I'd been with you after I'd been with Kyle.

"I kept thinking that I'd picked you knowing full well what things with Kyle had been like. I must have loved you even more than I'd loved him. If we survive the fight with Mephistoles I want to read those journals—all of them. I want to find out what *our* life together was like."

"It's all there and most of the last several journals are all in English. You can read them, but part of me thinks that it won't make any difference, that you'll still pick my brother."

Tears started running down my face, but I wiped them away. Crying felt like cheating. It probably wouldn't have felt that way with Kyle, but it did with Jace. Jace had such a big heart that it was probably hard for him to fight with me and stay angry once I started crying.

"Do you not want me anymore, Jace?"

He gave me a sad smile. "I still want you, Selene, I just don't know if I can do this. You want to date Kyle and me at the same time. Kyle might be able to deal with you dating both of us since he doesn't actually remember what it was like to be with you. I don't have that advantage. I look at you and I see my wife. I know you're not, I know you're a different person with a completely different set of memories, but in my chest it doesn't feel like that. I'm not sure I'll be able to stand watching you head off on a date with Kyle."

"I'm so sorry, Jace. I didn't want to make a mess out of everything. The last thing I want to do is hurt anyone—you especially—I just felt like I owed it to myself to find out what things had been like before. Things just kind of happened after that. You have every right to hate me."

Suddenly Jace's arms were around me and I realized that I'd been wrong about this house. It wasn't the house that felt like home, it was Jace. Standing there wrapped in his arms was like coming home after a long trip. The trip might be new and exciting, but at the end of it all you were glad to be back home, glad to be back in a world that was perfectly suited to you.

"Jace, I—"

"Don't say that you've already decided, Selene. You may believe that right now, but you haven't—you don't know enough to make that decision. You've only known me for a few days, you can't possibly be ready to commit to the next few hundred years with me. Even if you believe it right now, it can't last. Eventually you'll start wondering what you've given up on, what you're missing out on. I wish there was another way, but I knew all along that there wasn't. That's part of why I was trying to keep you at arm's length before. I knew that I needed to tell you about Kyle before I could ask you to marry me again.

"I've spent a lot of time lately reading through my old journals, the ones from before you and I were together. It sounds like it was hard for me to see you with Kyle, that sometimes I wasn't sure if I could take another day of it, but in the end I never went anywhere. I knew all along that I wanted you in my life in whatever form I could get, even if that was just as my friend. I don't think that we could go back to that—too much has happened between Kyle and I since then—but I'll give you a chance to decide."

"I'm so sorry, Jace. You deserve so much better than this."

"Maybe. It doesn't really matter though—I've known since the first moment I saw you several hundred years ago that I was made for you, that I would never be happy with anyone else."

Chapter 25

I would have stayed there forever if I could, wrapped in Jace's arms, pretending to myself that my decision had been made, but time marched relentlessly forward. All too soon Kat showed up pushing a dolly that was loaded down with a massive metal case.

"That's all of them?"

"Yeah, everything including the two that Genevieve left in that box for you to give Selene when you found her. Mephistoles claims that he's on his way with Peter, but my bet is that he's already here watching us, waiting to make sure that we really leave with the journals. His accomplice, whoever they are, is probably bringing Peter."

Jace nodded absently, no-doubt thinking through contingencies. Finally, he sighed and patted the metal box.

"Okay, this is all new for you, Selene, but the real prize as far as Mephistoles and the other pantheons are concerned is this vault and the journals inside it. He's never going to even let us see your dad unless he really believes that the journals are outside the protection of our wards.

"Mephistoles wants us to believe that he's going to go through with the exchange if we give him the journals, but the truth is that he's going into this expecting to kill us so that he can bash down our wards and make sure we didn't hold anything back. It's just the way someone like Mephistoles thinks—your dad is nothing more to him than leverage that will let him pin us down so he can finish us off."

"This is all a huge mistake. I never should have asked the two of you—"

Kat cut me off before I could go any further. "This isn't all just about you, remember? We aren't going to leave your dad in Mephistoles' power. Besides, I'm well and truly sick of Mephistoles. He was a thorn in our side even before he got that stupid artifact, but he's gotten even worse since then. It's past time that we put him down."

The words were harsh, but I knew Kat well enough to know that she wasn't tearing into me. She was just functioning as best she could through a torrent of fear and anger.

The last of my concerns about her dating my dad melted away as I finally registered how hard this was for her. If she was willing to face her fears like this for him then she didn't just have my permission, she had my blessing.

I crossed the distance between us in two quick steps and wrapped my arms around her. "Thank you for doing this, Kat. I don't deserve you, but I'm glad you're here."

"Yeah, well, nobody really *could* deserve me so at least you're in good company."

Her voice carried more of the laughter and teasing I was used to from her, and hearing that was a little piece of coming home too. Some people went through their entire lives wishing that they had a family, but I didn't have just one, I had two, two incredible families that I didn't even begin to deserve. All I could do was give them all my best and hope that it would be enough.

I looked over and caught Jace smiling at the two of us. He saw me watching and his smile shifted from being for both of us to being just for me. Maybe things could still be okay between the two of us.

"Mephistoles won't risk destroying the vault, so we stay as close to it as possible to start out with. When Mephistoles tries to double-cross us, Selene stays next to the vault while Kregor, Kat and I carry the fight to him. Selene, you can throw an occasional sun lance his way, but keep an eye out. Sooner or later his accomplice will make a play for the vault and you'll need to be ready."

Bethany had been so silent for the last little while that I'd almost forgotten about her, but she suddenly buzzed in and settled on my shoulder.

"What if there are more than just two of them?"

I shook my head at her. "This isn't your fight, Bethany. You said it yourself a little while ago. You don't have enough power accumulated to survive being disembodied yet."

"This is my fight if I choose for it to be. I spent the better part of twenty years looking for you and then once I found you, I only got a couple of days with you before you disappeared. I'm not doing another twenty years like that. This is my fight too."

I closed my eyes for a second. We didn't have time for an extended fight, but I needed to make her see that there wasn't any point in throwing her life away like that.

"The next twenty years don't have to be like the last twenty years, Bethany. Jace and Kat can see you now. If the worst comes to pass you can find some other Awakened and hang out with them. You'll get to watch TV and talk to people."

"Yeah, fat chance of that. I'd just end up as a glorified gopher. No TV, just a lot of running around delivering messages with no prospect of getting any bigger for another twenty years until you come back in your next incarnation."

"Then don't go find another Awakened, go hang out with the Seelie Court."

"I can't do that!"

"Why not?"

Bethany looked embarrassed, like she'd said something that she shouldn't have. "I just can't.

Can we leave it at that? I'm coming with you and all this is doing is wasting time. What do we do if there are more than just the two of them?"

Jace and Kat exchanged looks and then shrugged. "We try to burn peak memories and take as many of them with us as possible. We can't win at that point so there's no use holding anything back."

Bethany rolled her eyes at him. "You suck at motivational speeches. Let's get this show on the road."

We left the house a couple of minutes after that. Kat and I carried one end of the vault while Jace carried the other. It would have been a simple matter for any one of us to amp up our strength and carry it by ourselves, but apparently we were all worried about depleting our emotional reserves.

We walked for more than a mile and a half through the forest, and I felt like I could feel Mephistoles' eyes on me the entire time. It was disturbing in ways that I hadn't been expecting. Kregor buzzed around, always within sight of the rest of us, but obviously making sure that we weren't going to walk into some kind of ambush.

It made a lot of sense. Kregor probably didn't want to be disembodied any more than the next guy, but he was old enough and powerful enough that it wouldn't be the end for him if it happened. Bethany, on the other hand, just rode on my shoulder with one hand knotted around a lock of my hair. I suspected that she was starting to second-guess her decision to come with us, but I wasn't going to call her out on it.

I couldn't blame her for being scared; I certainly was.

Three-quarters of the way to the rendezvous I realized that we'd been angling around a large hill. That was smart, it meant that Kat and Jace's house was less likely to be caught in the crossfire. That wouldn't matter if we all died in the next few minutes, but it meant that there was still a chance that we'd survive and get to go back to it once this was all over.

A few minutes later we dropped into a natural amphitheater. Mephistoles was waiting for us at the far end.

"You brought the journals?"

Jace hefted the vault a little higher and nodded. "You brought Selene's dad?"

"Open up the crate first."

"No. Show us Peter or we'll just turn around and go home."

Mephistoles gave Jace a cold smile and pointed back behind us. I turned and saw my dad standing there at the top of the hill with his hands tied in front of him. He looked tired, bruised and half-starved, but he was still alive, and that was such a relief that I almost didn't even register the identity of the person standing next to him.

I should have known that Sandra would end up involved with Mephistoles. Jace and Kat had been so insistent that she was nothing more than a mimicry, that the odds were just too steep against the two of us being born here at the same time, but part of me had refused to believe them.

Her dislike of me had been too instant, too strong to be anything other than something carried over from a past life. That was supposed to be impossible, but it was happening to me, so maybe it was happening to her too.

"You've seen him, now open up the vault and let me see the journals."

We set the vault down and Jace flipped the lid up. I didn't know what that was supposed to prove to Mephistoles other than that we'd crammed it full of a bunch of black, leather-bound books that might or might not be my old research journals, but his eyes got big, like an addict who had just spotted his next hit.

"Kill the father and take them!"

Everything exploded into violence with such speed that I would have been killed if not for the fact that I was standing so close to the journals.

Kregor darted up and to the side, his sword—little more than a long knife for some-one my size—held at the ready. Jace had left his ax with the Lady, but he instantly amped himself and drew his sword, dashing away to the right even as Kat moved the other direction.

Kat had grabbed a trio of short, throwing spears from the armory before we'd left along with a slender sword for me, and the first of the spears shot towards Mephistoles at more than a hundred miles per hour.

Jace and Kat hadn't held back at all on their augmentation. I finally managed to get myself amped up to about five times normal speed, but they were still moving faster than I was. I caught all of that out of the corner of my eye as I turned back towards Sandra and shot up the hill.

I'd wasted nearly a second trying to come to grips with the idea that Mephistoles had just casually ordered Sandra to kill my dad. I suspected that I was going to regret that delay.

There was a brief instant where Sandra didn't move—as if she'd been shocked by Mephistoles' order to kill my dad—but then she slammed the knife she was holding into his side and charged down towards me.

My dad crumpled, falling to his knees, but there wasn't anything I could do to help him. I didn't know how to heal, and my minuscule first-aid skills weren't going to keep him from dying. There was only one way to save him. I had to kill Sandra and then help Jace and Kat kill Mephistoles. If I was fast enough then maybe there would still be time for Jace to heal my dad.

Sandra cut loose with an attack that looked like a black shockwave made out of heavy smoke. I threw myself to one side, trying to get out of the way of the attack, but I wasn't quite fast enough. I managed to avoid the darkest part of the attack, but the fringes still caught me, and

I felt a section of my shirt tear away just above my right hip.

The pain didn't hit me until an instant later, but when it did it nearly brought me to my knees. I managed to keep moving, but it staggered me, stopping my forward progress, and that was bad enough.

"Keep moving, Selene!"

Bethany's yell and the feeling of her hand against my neck were the only anchors left for me to grab hold of, but they were just barely enough to keep me from going all the way down. I shot a sun lance at Sandra—more to buy myself time than because I actually expected to kill her with it—and pushed myself forward.

I didn't remember drawing my sword. It seemed useless given that both of us were capable of killing from a hundred yards away, but it was in my hand and I raised it into position as we clashed into each other.

It seemed impossible considering that just a few days ago Sandra had still been unawakened, but she was better at this than I was. The air in front of her pulsed and knocked my sword out of the way and then her knife licked out and cut me in the shoulder.

I reeled back away from her, nearly overcome by shock, but she didn't give me time to get set again. I caught a glimpse of the other fight as she closed again, moving almost as fast as I was. I saw Kat launch a sun lance at Mephistoles that the old man turned without noticeable effort in the split second before he launched a pulse of darkness like Sandra had just used on me.

Jace was faster than I was, but Mephistoles' attack covered easily twice the area Sandra's had, tearing a massive furrow in the ground along the bottom edge of the effect. Jace dodged to the right, but he wasn't going to be able to get all the way clear. My breath caught and then a pulse of white light cut through Mephistoles' effect, clearing a hole in the attack so that Jace could slip through it and continue forward towards Mephistoles.

The force of my sword hitting Sandra's shield had knocked it free of my hand, but Sandra's rush back towards me didn't leave me any time to arm myself with anything else. She slashed again—this time at my neck—but I finally understood what it was that I'd done wrong during our first exchange. I was faster than her, I needed to use that advantage rather than trying to slug things out in the kind of fight that Mephistoles excelled at.

I leaned back just far enough for her knife to miss me and then shot forward and slammed my hand into her stomach. I'd expected my attack to maybe double her over at best, but I was willing to take whatever strikes I could land on her—however ineffectual.

Despite the thick refusal of the air to fill my lungs like I wanted it to, I'd still somehow forgotten just how amped up my strength was.

My punch—poor form and everything—didn't just fold Sandra in half, it launched her backwards down the hill. It was devastatingly powerful. As she crashed into the ground, I realized that I probably would have paralyzed her if not for the fact that her bones and muscles were amped up.

I was so shocked that I forgot for a second to follow up on my attack. I remedied that a second later and ran down the hill towards her, but I'd waited too long. Sandra rolled with the impact from hitting the ground, and came up spitting mad.

She'd lost her knife somewhere along the way, so she launched another of the shadowy ripples at me. I was moving too fast to dodge, instead I threw myself upwards, sailing over the worst of the attack as I threw another sun lance at her.

This time I almost hit her with the bar of molten gold, but even as she dodged to her right she was moving exactly to where I wanted her. The shockwave from her attack had destroyed my shoes and the bottom third of my pants. The pain was once again intense. It felt like all of the flesh below my knees should have been torn off of my bones, but when I looked down it was all still there. It was bruised like someone had taken a baseball bat to me, but it was still there and still responding to my will.

My feet caught Sandra in the chest as I came down from my jump, and this time I knocked her into a tree that was more than six feet around. She mewled in pain as we both dropped to the ground and went rolling down the hill.

She probably should have come up on top, but was apparently too disoriented. I flipped her over and straddled her. I was going to hit her, but I caught a flash of movement and leaned back as her hand—glowing with some kind of crackling white energy—passed mere inches in front of my face.

I'd turned slightly to one side at the last second to try and buy myself a little more room, and was glad I had because even with a near miss, the energy surrounding her hand burned my skin. I screamed out in pain as the entire left side of my face felt like it had been set on fire.

I fought past the pain and grabbed her arm, trying to keep her fist away from me. I succeeded in slamming her hand into the ground, but all that did was cause an explosion of debris as her energy effect shredded the leaves and sticks under it.

The same effect blinked into existence on her other hand, but I'd been expecting that and I grabbed her left arm as well, pinning her arms above her head, squinting my eyes against the hail of fragments as her effect destroyed another patch of ground.

"You should just give up now, Selene. You've been off making out with Jace while I've been back here spending every spare minute practicing new effects. I'm a natural—you've been out-classed from the start and you didn't even realize it."

I opened my mouth to tell her to go to hell, but her energy field was expanding, working its way down her arms so that soon there wouldn't be anywhere for me to hold onto her. Right as the skin on my hands started to tighten up from the destructive power inching towards it, Bethany landed on my shoulder again and I remembered that this was about more than just Sandra and me.

The maelstrom of emotions that swept through me was like nothing I'd even believed possible. The rage that had been powering me doubled and then redoubled again, but even it was overshadowed by the happiness and love that raced through my being.

The love was easy—I loved my family and friends. The rage was easy too—I'd hated Sandra for years now, hated her with a fury that I'd kept hidden away even from myself for fear that it would break free and consume me.

The happiness was something else altogether. I didn't understand where the emotion was coming from until I realized that things didn't have to end the way that Sandra wanted them to. I might not survive, but I could still make sure that she didn't get up and go after Jace and Kat; I could make sure that Bethany made it out of here. I still had a chance to make a difference.

I reached for another peak memory, planning on building the same kind of heat that I'd used to kill the pooka, but what came in response was something different, a crackling energy that broke through me like a tidal wave and then surged off my skin at the precise instant that Sandra's effect was about to touch me.

I'd never learned how to create the effect she was using, but somehow that was exactly what I did. The two fields struck with power that tried to throw us apart, but we were each pressing towards each other with amped muscles that would have put an Olympic power lifter to shame.

"You're not taking this away from me, you bitch!"

The pure venom in Sandra's voice should have shocked me, but it didn't. Somehow I'd known all along that her feelings went beyond anything the rest of the world could have expected. Only teenage girls could feel emotion with complete abandon, and Sandra was a teenage girl with centuries of history egging her on, a teenage girl who'd spent the last decade hating me with every ounce of her being.

Sandra's field surged out from her entire body, becoming brighter and denser. The hillside around us seemed to explode. Fist-sized rocks, jagged from being shattered just a split second previously, flew at me with enough force to go through a car, but that was nothing compared to the destructive potential of the crackling field coming off of Sandra.

It should have torn me apart. It almost did, almost made my field flicker out. I reached for more power, hoping to be able to feed more memories into my effect, but expecting to find out that I was completely out of emotional reserve.

I was working a powerful time amp and all of the various effects that made that possible, and I'd already shot out two sun lances. There shouldn't have been anything else left, but when I reached for more memories they responded and effortlessly slid out of the invisible hole in my forehead.

What was going on was beyond burning a peak memory, it was beyond anything I'd thought possible, but I didn't analyze it, I just stoked the blue, arcing energies of my effect higher and higher.

It was like having my soul torn away. I could feel myself become thinner, more transparent...less. The memories that defined who I actually was streamed out of me like water from a fire hose, and it still wasn't enough.

The rage behind Sandra's eyes wasn't entirely sane, but she matched the strength of my field and pushed even harder. I responded in kind, offering up months of my life and then going back for more.

The stream of burning memories was more akin to the flow of a waterfall now. Months of my existence disappeared in fractions of a second and I knew that neither of us could maintain it for long.

The terrible energies that we'd released could have destroyed everything for miles. They should have...only they were mostly directed against each other. Even so, the results of the energy bleeding out to the side was still digging into the solid rock beneath us.

I'd begun shaking several seconds before, but that had been a purely physical thing. The trembling now moved inside of me—tried to vibrate my soul to pieces—but I refused to give up. Right as I hit my personal breaking point I felt something change. Something from the outside tip the balance in my favor.

Our fields grew to the point where I couldn't look at Sandra, couldn't even squint past the brilliance created where they intersected, but then they somehow synced up and I was able to see her again. I watched as her expression changed, watched as something behind her eyes started to fade away. If I'd been solely powered by rage I probably would have incinerated her as her field started to weaken, but there was more than just rage in the mix, and I found myself stepping the strength of my effect down as hers faded.

She fought until the very last instant, pouring everything left into her effects. She pushed until she was nothing but a hollow shell that looked up at me in confusion as both of our fields winked out.

I punched her in the face, but I did so with only a fraction of the force available to me.

Once I was positive she was unconscious, I stood up and looked around at the pit I was standing in. It was more than forty feet in any direction, a perfect half-sphere of bare earth and rock without even a hint of vegetation anywhere around.

I felt punch-drunk and confused, but I knew that there was something I was supposed to be doing, something important. I stumbled up the side of the pit, and I got the feeling that the only reason I was able to climb in the soft dirt was the fact that I was moving too fast for the dirt to give way.

I made it to the top of the hill and took in what looked like a scene straight out of hell. Things were on fire, trees had been uprooted, and rocks had been thrown dozens of yards. There was one island of untouched ground on one side of the amphitheater, but other than that everything looked like a war zone.

I saw three figures fighting down in the midst of all that destruction, and my first instinct was to help the underdog, to assist the old man who'd been ganged up on...only that felt wrong somehow. I watched as a massive rock was hurled through the air. It started near the old man, but accelerated with incredible speed towards the girl. She tried to dodge, but the ground underneath her feet betrayed her. She dropped to one knee and for a second I thought it was all over. In the next instant, a rippling field of translucent rings appeared in front of her and the rock ricocheted away as she dropped to the ground unconscious.

The boy shot forward, desperately trying to get close enough to the old man to stab him, and never saw the branches that stabbed him from the side. As the boy dropped to the ground, I expected the old man to go tend to his wounds, but instead the old man picked up another rock and sent it over so it was floating above the boy.

In that instant something broke free inside of me and I screamed as a bar of liquid golden light shot out of my hand. The bar swept through the rock, vaporizing it instantly, and then took the old man in the stomach.

A shimmering shield flickered into place, intercepting my attack. It bought the old man—bought Mephistoles—a couple of extra seconds in which to dodge, but he seemed to be moving in slow motion and it was a simple thing for me to track his movements and keep the golden beam focused on him until the shimmer disappeared. There was a flash as the bottom half of his body vaporized and then nothing.

I sprinted down towards Jace, moving with all of the speed my amped up body was capable of, and arrived at his side panting and out of breath. There was blood everywhere. The branch had gone completely through him before slamming into the ground, pinning him there like some kind of massive insect.

He looked up at me, blood bubbling from his mouth, and tried to smile, tried to tell me without words that it was all okay, that he forgave me for everything. I was shaking again, but this time it wasn't due to overuse of my abilities, it was because the emotions inside of me were just too strong to be contained inside of my body.

I felt a movement on my shoulder and realized that Bethany was still standing at my shoulder. A part of me wondered how she'd survived the maelstrom of energy that had been surrounding me, but mostly I was still focused on Jace.

"Save him, Selene."

"I can't—I don't know how to heal him. Maybe Kat can do it?"

It was stupid to sit there staring into Jace's eyes rather than running over to see if I could rouse Kat, but I was frozen there, unable to move. I'd been stressed beyond what I could endure and now my mind was shutting down.

Bethany took to the air and zipped off towards Kat.

"No, it's no good, she's out cold. It's got to be you."

I shook my head as Bethany landed on my shoulder again. "I can't. Healing is one of the most complex effects there is. If you mess it up even a little bit you're as likely to kill your subject as anything else."

"He doesn't have much time, Selene. There is nothing to lose now."

I nodded and gave Jace my bravest smile. "No matter what happens, I want you to know that I've loved you ever since you saved me after school on the day Sandra slashed my tires."

Jace's smile rose fractionally, but I could see that Bethany was right—he didn't have more than a few more seconds. I put one hand on each side of his chest and summoned every spark of love and happiness I had as I willed his body to repair itself.

For the longest second of my life nothing happened and then suddenly I felt a host of effects click into place inside my mind. The effects reached out to Jace and his body regenerated before my eyes. The ends of the branch dropped away as the main piece inside of him was absorbed and converted into the raw materials needed to rebuild all of the damaged organs and muscles.

Jace's smile smoothed into an expression that was less pain-filled and he managed a single 'thank you' before he lost consciousness. I wanted to scream. I'd saved Jace, but I didn't know how I'd done it, and I could feel my emotions guttering into uselessness. They were still there, still real, but they'd taken on the washed-out tinge that told me they weren't capable of powering anything.

I'd been depending on Jace to save my dad, but that wasn't going to happen now. The air around me went back to normal as my effects all faded away to nothing. I knew it would take me at least ten minutes to make it up to where Sandra had left my dad, but I turned and started walking anyway. I couldn't just leave him there, not when he might still be alive. I at least owed it to him to be there for the end.

I'd made less than ten steps before I saw a flicker that brought me around to find Kyle standing in the spot where Mephistoles had died.

"Hello, Selene."

"Kyle! My dad—he's at the top of that hill. Please, you have to heal him."

"I already did. I took care of him while you were still fighting Sandra, you were just too busy to notice me."

"I don't understand, I thought you weren't going to help us."

"I wasn't."

Kyle reached down and came up a second later with a necklace of heavy metal links, and I suddenly realized why he was here. Excalibur was at his hip, one of the most powerful artifacts in existence, but that was nothing compared to the power represented by the other artifact in his hand.

"You didn't come here to help, you came here for the necklace."

His face tightened in anger. "I came here to help you."

"Fine, prove it by giving me the necklace."

He'd been mad before, but that was nothing compared to the rage dancing behind his eyes now. His fist tightened on the necklace until his knuckles were white.

"I saved your father, and I saved you. When you were fighting with Sandra and you reached the end of your strength it was me who tipped the balance in your favor. Me. I saved you and then you in turn saved Kat and my brother. I violated one of my rules for you by letting that happen, and this is the thanks you give me?"

"No, you may have saved me, but you never meant to save Jace. You would have let him bleed to death. You were hoping that I wouldn't be able to save him."

Something changed in Kyle's expression, something I couldn't read, something important that I would go back in my memories again and again to try and identify, but which I never managed to understand.

"I'm not giving you this necklace. This is what I've needed all along to make my plans succeed. I was only researching because I never expected to actually be in a position to acquire a second artifact. The next time you see me things will be different, Selene."

Epilogue

I sat there in the wreckage of a hundred acres of beautiful forest for more than an hour before Kat and Jace regained consciousness, at which point we carried my dad, Sandra, and the research journals back to the house. I say we, but really it was Jace. Kat and I were tapped out, but Jace still had enough emotional juice to make several trips back to the house.

I was half afraid I wasn't going to make it back to the house under my own power, but I managed it—it just took me a while.

Ari was overjoyed when Kat let her out of the basement and she found out that Dad was okay and none of the rest of us had been killed saving him. The journals were all saved, although Jace later revealed that most of them had already been scanned and saved to a thumb drive.

It made sense to back up something that priceless, and digital files were a heck of a lot easier to move around than a box full of books, but I would have liked to know that before we went into a fight against Mephistoles that we should have lost. It wouldn't have made any difference—Mephistoles still would have tried to kill us, but it still would have been nice to know beforehand.

My dad awoke to find Kat waiting at his bedside. He looked like he was still trying to process everything that had happened and everything he'd learned, but he wasn't freaking out and it was nice not to have to lie to him anymore.

I'd half expected Kat to jump into bed with him as soon as he was awake, but she was a lot more patient than I'd been prepared to give her credit for. She was moving with glacial slowness, but I could already tell that one day my dad was going to wake up and realize that he couldn't imagine a life without Kat. Convincing a guy like my dad to date someone who looked like she was seventeen—regardless of her actual age—was going to be a herculean challenge, but I had a feeling that Kat was equal to the task. She'd had a lot of years to practice her technique.

Kat and Jace seemed shocked that I'd left Sandra alive. To be honest, I was too. After more than a decade of her making my life miserable and then nearly killing my dad, I would have probably been justified in killing her, but I just couldn't bring myself to do that, not when the person who had stabbed my dad was truly gone.

IMMORTAL

I still couldn't look at Sandra without gritting my teeth, but I was dedicated to the idea of trying to reform her and make her a useful member of our pantheon. Four was still smaller than a lot of pantheons out there, but it was bigger than some, and it was infinitely better than two or three. Sandra would be starting from zero, but that would change over time, and simply having her around would go a long ways towards scaring off some of the groups that otherwise would have considered us easy pickings.

With Mephistoles dead, there was every reason to believe that we could remain off of everyone's radar for quite a while still, which was good; we all needed some time to recover.

Bethany was bigger than she was before our massive throwdown with Sandra and Mephistoles, but still not as big as Kregor. She'd absorbed a ton of the expended power since I was mostly using happiness as my driving emotion during the fight, but it was going to be a while still before she could risk being disembodied without truly dying.

Speaking of being disembodied, Kregor was obliterated early in the battle, but coalesced sometime the next day and made his way back to the house. Jace pretended not to be worried, but it was obvious to me that he was getting antsy by the time his sidekick rejoined us.

Only two things were really bothering me, and one of them wasn't even a bad thing. During the course of my fight with Sandra I'd drained her dry of memories. Normally I shouldn't have been able to do that without coming away equally drained. The fact that even my memories from before the time I'd been awakened had crystalized changed the math, but I still hadn't lost as much as I should have. I should have lost half of my memories, but instead I'd only lost about the first five and a half years.

That was still a lot to use at once—not enough to create another fairy, even if Bethany hadn't been there—but a lot still. A lot of it was probably just time spent wishing I could crawl or trying to learn to walk, but I still missed it. In one fell swoop I'd lost almost half of the memories from my time with my mom.

That scared me even more than I'd thought it would. I've had unlimited access to my old journals and plenty of free time for several days now, but I hadn't started reading them yet. It was more important to get everything else I remembered down in writing first.

I was also worried about what Kyle would do next. None of us were surprised when we got a message from the Lady two days after the battle. Apparently Kyle cleaned out Mephistoles' lair in record time and then dropped off the map completely.

Saying that the Seelie Court was unhappy to find out that Kyle now had both Mephistoles' necklace *and* Excalibur was pretty much the understatement of the year. I expected it was just going to be a matter of time before the Lady had the wards around Kyle's bunker pulled down, but I already knew she wasn't going to find anything important there.

Kyle was out there somewhere planning his next move, and no matter how many hours I spent going back over my last words with him, there wasn't anything I could do to change the past. It's very possible that things would have been different if I'd reacted differently, but it's too late to go back and change any of that now.

All we could do was wait and see what happened next.

Acknowledgements

Nearly all of the usual suspects need thanked again—I hope that you'll humor me as I do so.

As always, RJ Locksley and Amy Jirsa-Smith did great work on the editing side of things catching countless errors and suggesting subtle changes that ultimately made the book a much better story.

My team of advance readers continue to be much better than I deserve. A big thanks to Jenine, Janelle, Mei, Heather, Merissa, Mimi, Mom, Dad, Shalese, Matthew, Lachele and Kim.

Finally, I most definitely couldn't have done this without help from my wife, Katie. Not only is she my first reader and cover artist, she also supports me in a hundred other ways. If we have the year we're hoping to have in 2015, it will be as much her victory as it will be mine.

About the Author

Dean Murray is a prolific author with dozens of titles across multiple pen names and more than half a million copies of his work currently in circulation.

Dean started reading seriously in the second grade due to a competition and has spent most of the subsequent three decades lost in other people's worlds.

Things worsened, or improved depending on your point of view, when he first started experimenting with writing while finishing up his accounting degree. These days Dean has a wonderful wife and two lovely daughters to keep him rather more grounded, but the idea of bringing others along with him as he meets interesting new people in universes nobody else has ever seen tends to drag him back to his computer on a fairly regular basis.

Keep up to speed on Dean's latest projects at deanwrites.com.

Stone Heart

Dani's new home isn't just another stopover in a long chain of places she'll never see again, it's the home of both Caine and Jerek, two guys like nobody she's ever met before. One represents the best friend she's been hungering for, and the other represents something much more.

It should be the perfect recipe for a fairytale, but Caine and Jerek live in a dark, shadowy world and one of them is hiding secrets that will change everything, secrets that relate directly to Dani.

The Society

People need to be monitored, or they'll repeat the mistakes of the Desolation, a centuries-old war that killed billions of people and destroyed civilization.

Skye is part of the Society, the hi-tech, nanite-endowed group responsible for making sure that the millions of surviving people—grubbers—are confined to the ancient, decaying cities where they can be watched to ensure they aren't redeveloping the weapons technology that came so close to extinguishing life on the planet.

When the Society's monitoring programs pick up troubling developments in one of the grubber cities, Skye is ordered in to deal with the man responsible, but what—and who—she finds once she arrives will change everything.

Broken

Adri Paige's arrival in Sanctuary thrusts her into a dangerous, shadowy world most people don't believe exists, and places her in the middle of a war between darkly handsome Alec Graves and charismatic Brandon Worthingfield that threatens to consume the entire town.

On the surface, both Alec and Brandon are nothing more than average high-school guys, but as Adri is pulled ever more deeply into their conflict she realizes that one of them wants to kill her. Adri needs to decide who to trust before her time runs out once and for all.

The Greater Darkness:
(Writing as Eldon Murphy)

Something powerful is stirring in the darkness. Something so ancient that even creatures who've been alive for hundreds of years have long since discounted this new threat as nothing more than myth.

Normal humans will be caught in the crossfire, but then that's always the way of things. Geoffrey has no memory of his past life or any idea how to survive in the violent, dangerous world in which he's trapped. Despite his best efforts, he's about to find himself in the middle of a conflict that threatens to sweep away everything, and everyone he's been fighting so hard to protect.

CHET:
Whispers From The Past
By Larry Murray

30 years ago Charles Tucker lost everything that made life worth living. A brutal car accident killed his son. A short time later painful cancer took his wife.

The arrival of the Saunders family casts Charles' life into turmoil, tearing open unhealed wounds. Without his help the Saunders' financial troubles threaten to destroy them, but helping them risks destroying everything Charles spent a lifetime building.

Over all the turmoil looms Chet, the battered old '64 Chevy pickup that carried Charles' son to his death. For 29 years Charles blamed the old pickup for his devastating losses, locking Chet away in an old barn.

The most intriguing mysteries refuse to stay locked up. Solving this one promises an enchanting adventure for the whole family.

www.ingramcontent.com/pod-product-compliance
Lightning Source LLC
Chambersburg PA
CBHW030957260626

47169CB00002B/582